W9-BWR-969

3 5674 00622924 0

A PRIVATE VENDETTA

ALSO BY RODERICK GRANT

FICTION

The Dark Horizon (with Alexander Highlands)
The Stalking of Adrian Lawford
The Clutch of Caution

NONFICTION
Adventure in My Veins
Seek Out the Guilty
Where No Angels Dwell
Gorbals Doctor
The Lone Voyage of Betty Mouat
The 51st Highland Division at War
Strathalder: A Highland Estate

A PRIVATE VENDETTA

A NOVEL OF SUSPENSE

≥ ≥ ≥ ≥ ≥ ≥ ≥ ≥ ≥ ≥ ≥ ≥ ≥ ≥ ≥ ≥ ≥

Roderick Grant

Charles Scribner's Sons ≥ *New York*

Copyright © 1978 Roderick Grant

Library of Congress Cataloging in Publication Data

Grant, Roderick, 1941–
   A private vendetta.
   I. Title.
PZ4.G7728Pr   [PR6057.R323]   823'.9'14   78-14574
ISBN 0-684-15801-9

A PRIVATE VENDETTA

≥ ≥ ≥ **1**

⩾ ⩾ ⩾

Hate has the power to destroy a man, totally consume him, to eat at his soul like a cancer until there is no reason left, only thoughts of evil. When hatred becomes an ally of revenge the mind excludes reason and tolerance. Inside one's body there burns a fire so intense that only the culmination of the vendetta can extinguish it completely.

I know; I speak from the depths of experience. It has happened to me.

And now, as a result of my campaign of vengeance against those I had come to loathe, it is happening to me again. Only this time the roles are reversed. I am now the object of the vendetta. It is I who must cringe at every hint of danger; it is I who must live in the constant shadow of fear.

It is with me every morning when I leave home to go to my city office. It is there on the commuter train rattling into London; on the underground system, on the crowded tube trains, and in the warren of tunnels and escalators burrowing far below the city. Even in my office, shielded though I am as chairman and managing director of the firm and surrounded by secretaries and personal assistants, this fear is still present. It continues to haunt me when I return by train

13

each evening, then drive along the narrow country lanes to my home on the fringe of a Hampshire village. The times are few when it leaves me. Such is its power and intensity, so great the effect on my life, that there are moments when I feel it has always been part of me.

I live constantly with the crawling apprehension that my life is being subjected to an invisible scrutiny, that my every move is being shadowed and noted until, when the time is right and there is no possibility of any further mistake, they will move swiftly to kill me. I have outwitted them once. Try as I might, there is no certainty I can do so again.

≥ ≥ ≥

I knew they had found me when, one Saturday morning at the end of June 1975, I found Dodo, the family's pet donkey, dead in the paddock behind the outbuildings surrounding my house. The animal's throat had been cut and the letter T carved crudely in the flesh of his left flank.

Fortunately, it was early in the morning; I was the only member of the family up and about. It was a few minutes before six o'clock when I found the body lying close to a hawthorn hedge that bounds one side of the paddock. The body was cold and partly stiff, the blood around the wounds congealed to a thick, ugly crust. I knelt in the grass beside it, ignoring the dew that soaked my knees, momentarily stroking one of the long, silky ears. The sun was warm on my neck and shoulders but inside I felt cold, a numbness of mind and body that was both anger and fear.

I came to my senses within minutes. The body had to be dealt with while there was still time. I used my car and a rope to drag Dodo to the edge of a nearby wood on my land, and there in a sandy pit I buried him. At breakfast I told my wife and two young children that Dodo had died, that age had at last caught up with him. They appeared to believe me, but I knew they were puzzled by the speed with which I had disposed of the donkey without first giving them one last chance to see the body of an old and faithful family friend.

Five days later, while I was driving home from the station after a

14

tiring day in the city, the windshield and rear window of my car were shattered only half a mile away from my house. I explained to my wife that stones flung from beneath the wheels of a passing tractor had been responsible. But I knew without doubt that a bullet had caused the damage. I could not be certain, however, whether a serious attempt had been made to kill me—and had failed—or the single shot had been fired simply to warn and frighten me—a harbinger of the doom about to come.

Toward the end of the following week I entered the garage one morning to find the tires of my car slashed. Hanging from a door handle was a roughly cut piece of cardboard with the letter *T* scrawled in red paint. Some paint had splashed onto the concrete floor. The stains were like drops of blood. I could have taken my wife's car, but this would have involved explanations and, of course, there was no way I could have prevented her from seeing the damage for herself. So I drove on the rims to the garage on the other side of the village where the previous week the windshield and window had been replaced. I got a strange look from the proprietor, but he's one of those individuals who never pries unless information is volunteered. I said nothing beyond pointing out the extent of the damage and requesting that he do the job himself. He did not ask any awkward questions but instead drove me to the station, and when I returned in the evening, there was the car, with four brand new tires, awaiting me in the lot.

Later that evening I decided that steps had to be taken—and taken swiftly—to protect my family. My suggestion of a holiday in Spain for Felicity and the children—Mark and Ian, twin boys aged nine, now at home from school—was accepted with alacrity. I stressed that I would follow in a couple of weeks' time when the pressure of work lifted.

Felicity saw nothing unusual in this sudden whim on my part. After ten years of marriage she is familiar with my impulsive behavior.

I am a wealthy man, thanks to a thriving export and import business, and Felicity has always enjoyed sharing in the sometimes considerable financial rewards. Hard work—and luck—have brought riches, which include the large country house with twelve acres of grounds in Hampshire and another house and even more land in Spain. So she accepted the unexpected suggestion without demur and after two days, during which all remained uneventful, I saw them off at Heathrow Airport. I now breathed more easily in the knowledge that what was certain to happen would be against me alone, and that I need have no fear of their being maimed or even killed.

It was useless even to think of enlisting the aid of the police. To have sought protection would have meant revealing what had led to this impossible situation. There would have been no way to avoid telling how the previous year I had killed three men, one in Cyprus, another in Greece, and a third—the most despicable of the Tengerakis brothers—in London. In the eyes of the police I would be no more than a cold-blooded killer. In my own eyes and on my own conscience there is no such feeling. What I did was an act of retribution, an act of justice to avenge the foul murder of my younger brother Jonathan at their hands in a Cypriot village.

I waged my private vendetta against them and succeeded. But for one mistake, a flaw I could not have foreseen, I might even have succeeded in ensuring the secrecy of my mission, remained immune from discovery. However, the error, slight though it may have been, was made, and now the vendetta is in reverse. I am now the quarry, trapped in a situation entirely of my own making.

Theirs too is a private vendetta. They too are compelled to act by the same destructive forces that sent me in pursuit of revenge. Like lovers we are linked, drawn to each other by an invisible bond. But in this case the bond is one of hate and the chain of events like the unfolding of a curse.

Only death—my death—can sever the link between us. Only then will the curse be lifted.

⟩⟩⟩2

≥ ≥ ≥

It had taken me about a month to decide on a course of action following the news of Jonathan's murder in Cyprus. At first, when the official telegram arrived, my main reaction was one of shock; I was stunned. But after the pain and the heartbreak had established themselves and I had gone over again and again in my mind the circumstances of his death, I felt sickened, then possessed by a creeping paralysis of anger.

There had been only a small item about his death in a couple of the national daily newspapers. My morning paper carried the story on an inside page among its foreign news under the heading ARMY OFFICER DIES IN CYPRUS. It was an agency report datelined Nicosia.

The body of Lieutenant Jonathan Barker from Denborne in Hampshire was found today in countryside close to the Cypriot village of Berengaria near Limassol. A spokesman for the United Nations Peace-Keeping Force in the island, of which Lieutenant Barker was a member, said that the officer had been shot in the head and back. No direct motive was apparent, he added, although there was considerable unrest in Cyprus at the present time. It was possible that Lieutenant Barker, who

19

was wearing civilian clothes, had inadvertently strayed into the area during an exchange of fire between Greek- and Turkish-Cypriot gangs. The spokesman refused to confirm that the body of the army officer showed evidence of torture.

Jonathan's body was flown back to England by the RAF. The funeral was largely a military affair attended by many of the officers from his regiment. There were few relations present because, quite simply, there are few close relatives. Jonathan and I had no sisters. There was twelve years' difference in age between us. When I was fourteen and he was two, our parents were killed in a car accident. Grandparents took on the responsibility of bringing us up. Now they too were dead. When Jonathan was murdered he was only twenty-two and I was thirty-four. Somehow his death made me feel like an old man.

It was a gray March day when we buried him. Large black clouds rolled across the sky, swept along by a strong wind that bit like the thrust of a knife. Everyone shivered, and throughout the slow walk from our village church to the graveside the rain poured down, adding misery to misery.

Behind the churchyard was a small hill, the slopes and the summit crowned by massive, aging beech trees. Rooks were building their nests high up amid the writhing, skeletal branches. Their incessant cawing partially drowned the ritualistic words intoned by the vicar as the coffin was lowered into the grave. I looked up and saw through my tears and the flurry of raindrops hammering on my face the dark birds twisting and turning, rising and falling, buffeted by the wind. The sight of them, black and somber against the stormy sky, filled me with a deep sense of foreboding; for a moment I hated them. It was as if something evil was there amid the swollen clouds. When I looked away and back toward the grave, the vicar was sprinkling earth on the lid of the coffin, and I tried to pray.

≥ ≥ ≥

Almost three weeks after the funeral the letter arrived. Up to that time, although the hate for my brother's killers was simmering within me, I might have been content to allow the scars to heal, to

20

dismiss as mere emotion any thoughts of my going to Cyprus to find out the truth for myself. The letter, written in a bold, clear hand, changed all that.

Inside the blue airmail envelope were three sheets of notepaper, the handwriting covering all six sides. There was no address at the top of the first page, and at the end the letter was unsigned.

Dear Mr. Barker,

You will be surprised to get this letter. I hope it will not come as too much of a shock. But after thinking things over I had to write because I know how close Jonathan and you were as brothers. He often talked about you when we were together. The official word here in Cyprus is that Jonathan's murder was a political killing—that he got in the way of rival groups of Greek and Turkish Cypriots. That is a lie because only I and the three men who killed him know the truth.

Your brother was murdered for two reasons—because he loved me and because he was a British soldier. In that sense I suppose it was a political murder. But really it was no more than a murder of jealousy. The men who did it are thugs, common criminals. They have killed before, in support of EOKA. They are ruthless and without mercy.

I know, Mr. Barker, because I was there when Jonathan was murdered. When they came for him we were together at my home. He had been warned about seeing me because one of the men who killed him believes that my family has pledged that I will marry *him*. I never wanted to marry any man except Jonathan. He was a kindhearted and gentle person. I have never loved anyone as much as I loved him.

He was killed by the beast I am expected to marry and by his two brothers, who are equally loathsome. I have vowed now that I will never marry him despite what my father has to say. How could I? But he is still determined. He intends to go to London to "make money," as he says. And when he returns to the island he will make me his wife. That is what he says, what he boasts about.

They took us both to a farmhouse where they said I must watch what was going to happen because this would be a lesson to me for daring to flaunt myself with a British officer after knowing that one of their own intended to marry me. I will never forget that night. I never knew until then that people could be so cruel. Let me say that all Greek Cypriots

21

are not of this nature. This family to whom the brothers belong is very large, the most powerful in the district, but they are mere peasants steeped in the ways of the past, people who use force to dominate any who oppose them. When you dare to offend one, you find you have offended all.

I feel you have a right to know these things—to know the truth. Also it is doing me some good in my mind to tell someone about this awful thing. I dare not go to the authorities—the police—not just because they forced me to swear I would tell no one, but because if I did I would be in constant fear of my life. Even if the three brothers were put in prison for the terrible thing they did, other members of the family—and there are many—would see to it that I paid the penalty for my folly.

I say again that I loved Jonathan deeply and sincerely. It makes me sad and ashamed of my people that there are vile creatures among them who could destroy someone like him who wished them no harm.

Forgive me for remaining anonymous. I hope you will understand.

I read the letter several times, and when I had laid it to one side there were only two thoughts in my head: a wave of revulsion for the manner in which Jonathan had met his death, and an overwhelming desire to find out more, not merely about the circumstances, but also about the three brothers who had murdered him; three figures, faceless and without names, who lived on an island two thousand miles away.

I was then confronted with the first of the snags. How could I trace the girl? I did not even know her name or where she lived, but I had to find her before I could do anything. I looked again at the envelope, but the postmark was blurred and covered only a part of the Cypriot stamp. Then I thought of Jonathan's personal belongings, three boxes of which had arrived several days previously.

I left the house and crossed the courtyard to one of the outbuildings, where the boxes had been stored. When they had arrived I'd felt unable to open them straightaway. Now I had no such qualms. Fortunately I could work undisturbed, Felicity having gone to London for the day and the daily help, Mrs. Tasker, not at work because of some family illness. With a pair of pliers I cut through the wire

22

bands fastened around the boxes. The tops were secured by nails and screws, so I pried off the boards with a screwdriver and a short iron bar.

The first box was filled with clothing and shoes, but in the second there were some letters tucked among books and magazines. I glanced at them, but they were a mixture of business correspondence and letters from army colleagues. The third box, smaller, contained a camera, more books, a writing case, and a photograph album.

I sat on an overturned bucket and leafed through the pages. There were several photographs of Jonathan in army uniform and a few of Salisbury Cathedral and Stonehenge, taken when he had been stationed in Wiltshire. Most of the pages, however, were filled with photographs, black-and-white and color, of people and places in Cyprus. He had always been interested in architecture, and there were numerous shots of monasteries and excavated Roman buildings showing pillars and arches and intricate mosaic floors. A couple of pages were devoted to views of the open-air Roman amphitheatre at Curium on the south coast of the island, and there was one particularly striking shot taken from the heights of the top tier of seats. In the foreground was Jonathan's profile looking down across the arena to the plain, hundreds of feet below; in the distance the slanting rays of the sun reflected on an indigo sea.

Toward the back of the album there were some more color photographs of Jonathan. They all appeared to have been taken at the same place, a cove with high cliffs and a wide stretch of sandy beach. In most of the photographs Jonathan—seated, standing, and in one, leaping into the air with his arms flung wide on either side—was laughing. In his blue swimming briefs he looked very fit and extremely handsome, his skin burned a deep shade of brown by the sun, his fair hair almost bleached to blond. Above all, it was obvious that he was very happy. For a moment my hands shook as I stared at the photographs. They trembled because of my heartbreak and the futility of a young life cut short in such a despicable fashion; they trembled as the rage mounted within me and my hate became more finely honed than before.

23

Throughout the album I came across several photographs of various girls, a number, judging by the backgrounds, taken in Cyprus. Obviously, with his good looks Jonathan had had no shortage of female admirers. A casual glance was sufficient to tell me none of them was the person I was seeking. Despite their sun-tanned faces and bodies, they were English girls, no doubt the daughters of service people or British residents on the island.

I turned the pages and there, right at the back of the album, were some photographs of a Cypriot girl. She was small and rather beautiful with glossy black hair and a flashing smile. No sun tan had given that sheen to her honey-colored skin. It was definitely the real thing. But more than any other factor it was her features, sharp and clearly defined, the nose and the rounded cheekbones, that spoke of her Mediterranean origin.

In several photographs she was standing beside a whitewashed building. It might have been a house; I couldn't tell. Only a part of a wall was visible. In others there was a vineyard in the background with what could have been the farmhouse far away in the distance. One showed the quay of a tiny harbor where fishing boats were clustered together like moths around their mooring bollards, and to the right were brightly painted houses and some children playing around a water pump in the center of the street. The remaining photographs had obviously been taken on the same stretch of beach where Jonathan was pictured on the previous pages. In these pictures the Cypriot girl was clad in a black bikini that emphasized her delicate and well-proportioned figure. The final two photographs showed her head and shoulders, and in both she was laughing, mouth open, white teeth glinting. But behind the almost childish, pleasurable gleam in her eyes, fastened firmly on the lens, there was no mistaking the expression of love for the man behind the camera.

Yes, this was the girl. My elation was quickly tempered with disappointment as I saw there was no name beneath any of the photographs. I placed the album on the floor and rummaged through the rest of the things in the box. I found Jonathan's wallet tucked inside a cardboard box that had once contained a jigsaw puzzle and now held postcards of views of Cyprus. The wallet was crammed with various oddments, and at the front, in the small pocket for holding postage stamps and tickets, were two small snapshots. I pulled them out. They were fading a little, slightly tattered and brown at the edges, but although the face depicted was that of a teen-age girl, there was no mistaking the features. It was the same girl. And on the back of each one, in the same firm handwriting as that on the letter I had just received, were the words "Love from Maria."

I began to feel happier. Now, at least, I had a Christian name to go on, although, heaven knows, when I thought about it I began to appreciate that there must be hundreds, perhaps thousands, of girls called Maria in Cyprus. All the same, I was making progress. Elated by my success, I started to make a thorough search of Jonathan's writing case. It was not long before I found what I had hoped would be there—two letters and a postcard, all signed "Maria." Unfortunately, none bore her address, but they were all postmarked Limassol. Judging by what she had to say in the letters, she had been very much in love with Jonathan; but it was the brief message on the postcard that provided me with my best clue.

Sorry I will not be able to meet you on Friday evening. I am taking my class to see some new excavations at the Palace of Vouni. As you know, it is a long journey and I will be tired what with this and coping with the children. Last time the bus broke down. I wish you could come too and be with me because I know how much you enjoy exploring Vouni. Please telephone on Saturday morning. All my love, Maria.

I now felt more than satisfied with my morning's work. Now that I had discovered she was a schoolteacher, most likely in Limassol, I knew it would not be too difficult to trace her once I got to Cyprus. I had made up my mind. No longer were there any lingering doubts about what I intended to do.

First I would find Maria and talk to her to learn the names of the brothers who had killed Jonathan. After that, I would plan on a day-to-day basis, taking things as they came, confronting situations as they developed. I would then establish the truth. Nothing less would satisfy me. There would be no need for any subterfuge about my trip

25

as far as Felicity was concerned. My exporting firm did a large amount of business with firms in Cyprus. It was two years since I had been out there.

I chose two of the best color photographs of Maria—one close-up and the other a full-length shot with the vineyard and farmhouse in the background—and slipped them into my pocket along with the postcard from Limassol. I went out into the sunlight and stood for a time in the middle of the courtyard letting the sun warm my face and neck.

Close to the house a group of cherry trees were white with blossomlike wreaths of snow glinting against the blue of the sky. From the wood behind the paddock, where I could see Dodo the donkey grazing with two of the ponies, came the echoing call of a cuckoo. A great sense of peace washed over me and for a moment I was lost amid the beauty of my surroundings and the fresh, intense feeling of hope that always comes with the first real day of spring.

I was made aware of just how much I worshiped this place, of how deeply I loved my home and my wife and children. Everything had gone well for us. It would be foolish to embark on some venture that might obliterate this happiness we shared. Was I about to take the first step toward self-destruction? Then, in my mind's eye, there came a vision of Jonathan, cheerful and gentle and vibrant, and I thought, too, of the unhappy girl who mourned him two thousand miles away.

In that instant I became tense and unhappy. Deep inside I felt a knot of pain that made me tremble and start to hate once again.

≥ ≥ ≥

Some weeks later, at the beginning of July 1974, I flew to Cyprus on a British Airways Trident. Normally I am bored by flying, despite the frills and extra luxuries offered by rival airlines to entice you to join them. On this occasion, however, the four-hour flight was a pleasure. While talking to one of the hostesses, I discovered that the captain was a Scotsman called Matheson with whom I had once shared a hotel—and a number of expensive drinking sessions—in Nairobi during a three-day strike at the airport. The hostess passed on my name and I was invited up to the flight deck.

Although, as I've said, I find flying as a passenger a tedious experience, I am enthralled by the technicalities of flight and the sheer complexity of the equipment that keeps a modern airliner in the air. Once I was installed on the flight deck, with Captain Matheson explaining this and that and a dozen other things besides, my boredom vanished. We were flying at around thirty thousand feet, and the blue sky encircling us, a sky that had looked so uninteresting only minutes before, took on a new dimension. While we talked I watched the other members of the crew seated at their positions. They looked relaxed and confident and laughed aloud once or twice when Matheson made one of his frequent jokes.

I stayed there for a good part of the remainder of the flight, watching the fluffy tops of the clouds glide beneath us as we flew on down the coast of Italy, then out high above the Mediterranean. Shortly before Matheson began to prepare for the approach to Nicosia Airport I offered my thanks and returned to my seat. I listened to the changing notes of the engines as the Trident descended. Within minutes I could see through my window, close to the port wing, farms and houses, fields, a monastery high up on a hill, clusters of villages, then the sprawling whitewashed suburbs of Nicosia glaring fiercely in the early afternoon sun.

Waiting to meet me in the terminal building was Christos Charalambous, a Greek Cypriot who handled the Cyprus end of my firm's business. He wasn't an employee. He, too, had an export and import firm to run, and he acted for my firm as associate agent. He obtained business for us in shipping goods, mainly asbestos, chromium, plaster material, wine, and produce such as grapes, citrus fruits, almonds, and potatoes. In return he handled the documentation of cargoes, much of them machinery and tools, shipped by us from Britain to Cyprus.

It has long been the practice to denigrate the role played by firms such as ours. We are accused of being middlemen who unnecessarily raise the price of goods by simply doing what we do and taking too much in the form of commission for our trouble. But a nation's trading life is very much dependent on a multitude of people like

Christos and myself, who smooth the path for commercial and industrial firms with goods to sell in foreign countries. I'm not saying there are no black sheep in the business, but then there are few walks of life without them.

Before leaving for Cyprus I had decided to make the trip a full-scale business affair. By doing this I had no need to invent excuses and worry over conflicting stories told to my wife and subordinates at the firm. It also gave me a legitimate reason for being in the island should the authorities for any reason become interested in my presence. Naturally, I hoped I would not arouse any suspicions on their part. And, after all, anyone was entitled to ask questions. No one could prevent me from doing that—no one, that is, except the three men most directly concerned about the extent of the answers.

Christos greeted me with a broad grin and an enthusiastic handshake. I had known him for many years and we'd always got on well together even when mistakes had been made by one side or the other and business had suffered. In his early forties, Christos presented a picture of solid rotundity, an effect made all the more startling by his short height. Despite the heat he was dressed formally in his usual dark blue suit with dazzling white shirt and red tie. He looked balder than when I had last seen him, and I noticed the film of sweat covering the dark skin on the dome of his forehead. What remained of his black hair was glistening with oil.

"Good to see you again, Christos," I said. "You look the same as ever except, perhaps, for a few more inches around that spectacular waistline of yours."

He laughed and slapped his paunch.

"Hah, you see the results of good living. We have made some good profits for each other these past two years."

"Too true. I hope there will be plenty more."

"Ah, well, business is so-so at the moment. But who knows, perhaps your visit to the island will improve matters."

"Perhaps," I replied.

I saw my suitcase emerge from a hatch in the far wall and come trundling across the room on a slow-moving conveyor belt. I walked over and picked it up. Christos took hold of my briefcase.

28

"Where to now, Christos? What luxurious establishment have you set aside for my indulgence this time?"

"Why, the very best, Mr. Barker. I know that only the best will do."

I think every time I had met Christos he had started by addressing me as Mr. Barker. In correspondence he always called me such. As usual, I reminded him to call me by my Christian name, Richard. He smiled and shrugged his shoulders apologetically. I knew he would do his best to remember, but the formality reflected in his dress was ingrained in his character.

Outside the terminal building the heat was fierce, with the sun riding high in a sky of intense blue. I had forgotten to pack sunglasses, and already the glare from the sunlight and the reflections from the white buildings and rows of parked cars and buses were hurting my eyes. Christos noticed my discomfort. He immediately pulled off his own dark glasses and handed them to me. I protested, but he was insistent.

"Go on. Take them. You can buy a new pair for yourself in Nicosia."

Inside his car the seats were almost too hot to touch. Christos wasted no time in starting the engine and getting under way. Cool air flooded in through the open side windows. With my handkerchief I wiped the sweat from my face and forehead, dabbing at the runnels forming on the back of my neck. Once we had left the airport perimeter and were on the road leading to Nicosia, Christos glanced at me and said, "You will notice many changes in Cyprus since last you were here, Richard."

I looked at him. The round face that always appeared to wear a permanent smile was now pensive and solemn.

"Things look very much the same to me, Christos," I said, glancing at the landscape on either side of the road. The plantations of orange and lemon trees, the neat houses with their white walls and brightly painted windows and doors, here and there a newish red-tiled bungalow blending with its long-established neighbors amid the brown, rock-strewn soil—all this looked unchanging. Even the new buildings looked as if they had been there forever.

29

"It is not in the places you will see what I mean," replied Christos. "The changes have come about in the people, Greeks and Turks. There is much more bitterness now than ever before. We are more uncompromising with each other. Each side is deeply suspicious of the other's intentions. The tension caused by this atmosphere of mistrust is greater than at any time in the recent past."

"Do you think there will be more trouble in the island?"

Christos punched at the horn, which blared repeatedly as we passed a group of youngsters riding bicycles three abreast almost in the middle of the road. He shrugged his shoulders and his expression remained gloomy.

"Who knows? It would seem there has never been a moment without trouble in this island since the very beginning of time. True, we get a few years of comparative peace now and again, but there is always someone or some organization waiting for the opportunity to stoke the fire once more. In my time there has been EOKA, our independence movement; then, when independence from the British was finally achieved, what happened? The politicians started bickering among themselves. This quarreling, which started as a war of words, soon led to fighting. Then the Turks saw the opportunity to cause trouble, and there were bombings and assassination attempts on everyone connected with the government, up to Makarios himself. He calmed the situation, righted a number of grievances as best he could—he's clever and cunning at this sort of thing—but the troublemakers were not content. What happens? The bloody fools, the idle layabouts who have nothing to do all day but sit on their arses and talk political claptrap, start whining for *enosis,* union with Greece. And that's what has led to the present situation. On top all appears normal, but just under the surface the whole island is seething and simmering and far too many people are wishing to get at each other's throats—Greek against Turk, in many cases Greek against Greek."

"I hadn't realized the situation was as bad as that," I said. "You amaze me, Christos. To an outsider it's hard to believe that in an island as lovely as this there could be such a serious edge to life."

We were now in the center of Nicosia, driving past shops and offices and crowded pavements. Christos was weaving the car among the lanes of traffic, continually blowing the horn. There were cyclists, buses, taxis, and cars, and suddenly I was aware of the constant noise: the raised voices, the horns, the tinkling cycle bells, engines revving, gears clashing, exhausts throbbing, pedestrians shouting. It was one great cacophony, a form of frenzied madness. For a moment I forgot the doubts and uncertainties raised in my mind by what Christos had just said and allowed myself to become part of the surging, restless tide of life on every side of me.

My exhilaration faded and I returned to reality when I heard Christos say in a soft, almost indistinct voice, "Life has always been taken seriously in this island. Unhappily, it is now a matter of more serious concern than ever before. Yes, Richard, when you delve deeply enough you find it is very bad."

≥ ≥ ≥

The Hotel Imperial tried hard to live up to its illustrious name. Built at the height of British colonial rule, it bore all the hallmarks of nineteenth-century splendor. It had wide verandas with elaborately carved balustrades and turrets perched aloft on various corners, while inside the rooms were spacious and lofty, the ceilings a pattern of intricate cornices. A sizable piece of ground surrounded the imposing building, and there were lawns, rockeries, and fountains, with graveled paths crisscrossing the expanse. Here and there, planted in small clusters, were tall, slender cypresses, pinnacles of vivid green against the cloudless sky. Small birds beat their wings amid the dust in the pools of shade at the base of the trunks.

In the distance behind the high walls of the garden I could hear the throb of Nicosia's traffic and the occasional shriek of children at play. Almost above my head a pair of turtle doves cooed monotonously from their perch on the hotel roof. From the swimming pool directly in front there were shouts and bursts of laughter as a group of youths cavorted in the blue, translucent water and yelled encouragement to one who hesitated on the tip of the high diving board.

Christos's voice broke through my thoughts.

"It was indeed bad news about your brother. It made me very sad that such a terrible thing could happen."

We were seated close to the pool beneath the sprawling branches of a eucalyptus tree. I had slept for a couple of hours, then gone out to buy a pair of sunglasses and a postcard, which I had sent off to Felicity telling her of my safe arrival. Having arranged with Christos that he should have dinner with me that evening, I had asked him to come to the Imperial around six o'clock. We were enjoying the first of our predinner drinks, and although I had been expecting him to mention Jonathan's death, now that he had done so I felt a strong reluctance to talk too much about it. I had no wish to betray the intensity of my inner feelings.

Christos noticed my hesitation, mistaking it for grief. The ice cubes rattled against the side of his glass as he placed it on the low table between our chairs.

"I'm sorry, Richard. I did not mean to upset you by speaking of Jonathan. It was———"

"Please, Christos, don't apologize. Forgive me. I must have been dreaming. I've been waiting for an opportunity to thank you for the letter you sent after the news of his murder was released. I appreciated that very much. I was very touched."

Christos raised both hands.

"It was nothing. The very least I could have done. I only met your brother on one occasion, shortly after he came to the island, when he was based here in Nicosia. He was a very likable boy, interested in Cyprus and its history as well as present-day problems. I only wish I could have done more to help him through the maze that is Cypriot life today. Perhaps if I had been able to do something for him, he might still be alive. But he was posted to the south and we never met again."

There was a shriek, followed by a loud splash and a gust of laughter. In the pool I saw the youths crowding around the boy who had at last plunged in from the diving board. They were cheering and clapping him on the shoulders. To judge from their looks, they seemed to be a mixed party of Cypriots and Europeans and I briefly envied them their youth and exuberance, their totally carefree behavior. They were like a pack of young animals at play, proud and self-assured in their youthful innocence, unaware of the troubles of life.

Christos saw me looking at them as they clambered out of the

32

pool, tousled heads dripping, jostling and wrestling each other, then darting haphazardly across the terrace toward the showers and the changing rooms.

"Perhaps you see the image of Jonathan in one of those boys," he said softly.

"Yes," I replied. "In a way he was both one and all of them, although a few years older, of course. He too had good looks and an abundance of energy. Even when he matured, at heart he was still a boy. He loved life and lived it to the full."

"You were much older than he. Yet you were very close?" asked Christos.

I picked up my glass and held it with both hands in front of my face.

"Yes. Extremely close. I was married and had children while Jonathan was still in his early teens. We grew up—or he did—without our parents, so it was to me he turned whenever he was in trouble or had problems. I often had to put him straight and get him out of a jam, but he never resented my telling him off. In fact, in many ways I was both father and brother to him. It seemed to bind us even closer."

I finished what remained of my gin and tonic. The empty glass made a hollow ring on the marble table.

"Sometimes, I think I'll never truly appreciate the fact that he's dead. It seems such an impossible thing. I think the news was the greatest shock I've ever received. It affected me much more deeply than when I was told my parents had been killed in a car crash. But, of course, I was only fourteen then, and the young have no yardstick for measuring the extent of their sorrow."

Christos was looking directly at me when he said, "You told me on one of your previous visits that you saw Cyprus as a heavenly place, that the island's people were among the best you had known in your years of business travel around the world. Have those feelings been swept away by the tragedy? Have you become bitter toward us?"

"No, Christos. There's no point in my hating a place and a people. The bitterness, contempt, hatred—call it what you like—in

33

my heart is reserved for the person or persons who murdered my brother. There are men of violence among the decent people of every race."

Christos smiled and sunk his chin on his chest.

"Cyprus has a reputation for being a violent place. You are a forgiving man, Richard."

For a moment I felt humbled by the sincerity of his remark, but also ashamed because locked in my heart was the true reason for my being in Cyprus—my secret hate. It was then I remembered an earlier remark he had made.

"You mentioned that if you had known Jonathan better you might have been able to help him come to terms with Cypriot life. What did you mean, Christos?"

"Life can be very complicated in this island now. Ever since 1968 the enmity between the Greek and Turkish communities has been growing steadily. We are, in effect, two quite separate peoples attempting to control our own destinies, while at the same time, because Cyprus is a small place, we are continually forced into contact with each other. There is no avoiding this. Of course, the Greek Cypriot government under Makarios is the only legal administration in the island, but since that government participated in an economic blockade of one of the Turkish zones in 1968, the Turks have never forgiven them. They have ignored the government ever since because of that. They now have their own 'provisional administration,' as they call it, and although it's not legal under the constitution, it does act as a useful channel of communication between the Turkish community and the United Nations Peace-Keeping Force."

"But if the two communities try to lead separate lives and keep out of each other's way, where does the trouble come into it? How can there be conflict?"

"Apart from the absolute zones for the Turks—and only in a few of the larger towns do such ghettos exist—it is not possible for the communities to be completely independent of each other. There are many places, small villages and rural districts, where in fact the two live quite happily side by side—and have always done so—no matter what the political conflict. For the main part, Greek and Turkish

34

Cypriots come face to face in a variety of circumstances—at work, using the same roads, and in shops. Then there are those Greek Cypriots who want *enosis,* who are committed to seeing the island united with the Greek mainland, and, as far as I can see, an equal number who are totally opposed to such an idea. As a result they fight with each other. The Turks get caught in the middle. As they are afraid of any link with Greece, they are prepared to fight any person who is a Greek Cypriot simply to make known how they feel and to keep things as they are. And all the time there are rumors, sometimes every other day, every week, that Makarios will be overthrown with help from the Americans or the colonels in Greece. And if that should ever happen, no doubt the dictatorship in Athens will move swiftly to establish a true union of the island with Greece. Naturally, the Turkish government in Ankara would never stand aside and allow this to take place. They would invade as they have pledged to do time and again in the past. Then . . .''

He shrugged his shoulders. There was a wry smile on his face.

"Then truly the day of reckoning will have arrived."

"Is that day far off, Christos?"

"I don't know. Who knows? It is only possible to hope that it is—for all our sakes."

"But I still don't see how you could have helped Jonathan."

"I could have warned him to be wary of becoming too involved with either side, outside his official duties. Generally speaking, the UN force is respected by both Greeks and Turks. But there are still plenty of Greeks who do not like the British because of things they did during the struggle for independence. This is especially so in the country districts, where old habits and traditions die hard and the people have long memories. Bitterness has a habit of infecting the soul. For many of the older Greek Cypriots it is like a disease; their hate can never be checked or extinguished no matter how many years go past. That's why I fear Jonathan must have been imprudent in some way. But no doubt the truth will emerge one day. It usually does, although sometimes it is better not to know the truth. Don't you agree?"

I nodded, then beckoned across the terrace to a waiter.

35

"Let's have another drink before dinner, Christos. Then we must change the subject, talk of something else—something more cheerful."

Christos laughed, shoulders quivering, hands clasped across his huge stomach.

"Aha, then that means we must talk of business—of making money. For me, Richard, that is indeed a cheerful subject."

≽ ≽ ≽

Although I was impatient to get to Limassol to find Maria, I had to spend several days with Christos going through the motions of business: discussing statistics, profit margins, and tariffs, lunching with businessmen who wanted to increase their trade with Britain and other European countries, and meeting old, established customers who would have considered it discourteous had I failed to call on them.

In normal circumstances my mind would have been concentrated on the important matters at hand, but time and again throughout a series of discussions I found my attention wandering, my thoughts focused on the girl who had written to me and the three brothers who had brought grief and heartbreak to us both. Doubts and uncertainties continually preyed on my mind: would she be willing to talk freely to me? If so, how much would she be prepared to tell? How could I act on the information I hoped she would give to me? After having traveled this distance, would I even be able to trace her at all?

My brain was such a welter of churning thoughts that on one occasion Christos broke off his conversation to ask good-naturedly if I was still awake. I apologized at once.

"I'm afraid it's the heat," I said. "And we've been so busy these past few days. I haven't acclimatized myself yet."

Christos laughed.

"I thought Englishmen were at home in any climate."

"Not this Englishman." I yawned and stretched my arms above my head. "I am tired, all the same. We've had too many late nights."

36

"So," replied Christos. "But the late nights have been fruitful ones. Don't you agree?"

I nodded. Christos was a demon for work, and thanks to his persuasive and dogged manner we had succeeded in obtaining a considerable amount of new business which, in the long run, would benefit both of us.

"Yes," I said. "I can see you haven't lost your master touch—your ability to tackle the impossible and make it work. All the same, I think I'll take a break for a few days. I'd like to go south and look at the sights, spend some time up in the Troodos Mountains. My wife will never forgive me if I don't take some color slides with my new camera while I'm here. She gave it to me recently as a birthday present. It's dripping with gadgets. I'm sure I'll never be able to use it properly."

A despondent expression passed across Christos's features.

"Ah, what a pity you want to go this weekend. As you know, I have some appointments to keep and then there will be the arrangements for my nephew's wedding next week. You will come to that? Please."

I tapped him on the shoulder. "Of course. Don't worry. I'll be back in Nicosia on Sunday evening. That will give me three days with nothing to do but enjoy myself. When is the wedding?"

"In one week's time, on Thursday. But we'll be able to get down to work again on Monday and Tuesday after you return. On Wednesday I will be too busy coping with the family."

"You're a glutton for work, Christos. Take my advice and relax a little. You can't be in the office all the time."

He tidied the mass of papers on his desk. In the distance we heard the sonorous tolling of a monastery bell; closer, in the street beneath the window, the droning of traffic, and now and then a shout or a burst of laughter. Christos cocked his head to one side, listening for several moments to the relentless, mournful sound of the bell, then said without a trace of a smile, "In Cyprus, Richard, work is a panacea for forgetting the signs of trouble all around. It helps me ignore the rumors, the gossip, the daily intrigue. Work allows me to preserve my sanity; it keeps me happy when, so easily, I could be sad."

37

≥ ≥ ≥

I hired a car and set off for Limassol after breakfast Friday morning. It was a pleasant drive of just over fifty miles through farmland, groves of orange and lemon trees, and a rugged, boulder-strewn landscape interspersed with forests and rivers flowing through fertile, wooded valleys. Between the villages of Nisou and Kophinou, the monastery of Stavrovouni dominated the plains from its perch on the peak of a two-thousand-foot mountain.

I stopped the car and got out. Shading my eyes against the glare of the sun, I gazed up at the distant building. To look at it was like viewing some painting come to life from the pages of a history book. It was both fortress and aerie, and its long, squat shape appeared not to have been built but to have grown naturally from the heart of the peak with its massive crags and buttresses of rock. At the foot of the mountain and for some distance up the slopes were cypresses and pines, and in the still, almost heavy atmosphere, pungent with the scent of thyme and resin, the silence was absolute except for the droning of bees and the gurgling of a nearby stream.

I thought of the devout colony of monks, reputed to be the strictest religious brotherhood on the island, praying, tending their bees, and cultivating their vines, high above in their mountain stronghold with its uninterrupted views toward the Troodos Mountains to the west and the sea to the east. Here was the ultimate in peace and beauty, a scene from another age. For several minutes I stood and gazed at the splendid sight and tried to forget my own worries and fears and my hate.

This mood was abruptly shattered by a truck rounding a bend, then changing into top gear as it roared past me. The air was filled with exhaust smoke. Gone was the scent of herbs and trees. The smell of burning oil and the echoing noise pulled me back to reality and the twentieth century. I got into the car and drove off, accelerating rapidly, anxious to retain the picture in my mind.

On reaching Limassol I found a small hotel close to the seafront with a clear view of the harbor from my bedroom window. I sat for ten minutes watching the ships riding at anchor and tied up alongside the various wharves; I pondered the situation and made

38

things clear in my mind as to what I had to do. From now on I would have to tread warily, outwardly displaying no more curiosity and concern about the circumstances of Jonathan's death than what would be deemed natural from a close relation.

My mind made up, I went downstairs to the bar, had a couple of drinks, then put through a telephone call to the local headquarters of the United Nations Peace-Keeping Force. I explained my identity and was transferred to a Captain Fraser, with whom I made an appointment for two o'clock that afternoon. After a light lunch I emerged from the air-conditioned comfort of the hotel into the cloying afternoon heat and walked the short distance into the center of Limassol.

Fraser was a slim, red-haired man of about twenty-five. His face was extremely pale and his forearms, bare beneath his short-sleeved shirt, showed no traces of sun tan. A shy, nervous smile crossed his face as we shook hands, and I was close enough to see the freckles on his snub, boyish nose.

"When I telephoned earlier today I was told you had been a close friend of my brother," I said.

Fraser nodded.

"Yes. You could say that. There aren't many British officers in the Limassol division of the UN. Mostly Danes and Dutchmen. I suppose it was natural we should become friends. I liked Jonathan. He was a jolly nice bloke."

I smiled in an attempt to put him at his ease.

"It's nice of you to say so. And to take the time to see me at such short notice."

He motioned me to sit down, and I lowered myself into a squat, uncomfortable armchair directly underneath the window of his office. Fraser sat behind his desk and offered me a cigarette from a tin beside the telephone. I refused, and while I glanced at the maps of the island and detailed, large-scale diagrams of the various towns and major villages in the Limassol district that adorned the drab green walls, he snapped open his lighter and lit a cigarette for himself. He then sat bolt upright in his chair, elbows white against the desk top.

39

"Have you come all the way to Cyprus, Mr. Barker, to find out more about Jonathan's death?" he asked. "If so, then I'm not going to be a great deal of help. I know nothing more than you do, because I was on leave at the time and only read about it in the newspapers. It was a great shock. Of course, I read the official statement when I returned here. I expect you were given the same details."

"And do you agree with them?"

His only hesitation was to exhale a stream of smoke into the sun-filled room. It hung blue and heavy in the dusty air above our heads.

"Yes," he replied. "Jonathan was extremely unlucky. In our job we have to try to achieve an equal balance of fairness toward both Greek and Turk. It's terribly difficult, because at times both sides can be bloody awkward and stubborn when it comes to asserting their rights, or what they think are their rights. It may have been that Jonathan, who I know was well liked and respected by most, was thought by some of the Greeks to be more partial toward the Turks. It's not hard to create this sort of impression if you're prepared to listen to grievances and try to do something to help. And Jonathan did more than his share in this direction. Anyway, whatever the reason, he was killed near a village with a large Greek Cypriot population. That village has often been the scene of fighting and skirmishes in the past. It's very likely that the official version of the circumstances is correct—that he stumbled on a local feud and got caught up in the cross fire."

It would have been too easy at that stage—and too dangerous—to have blurted out some hint of what I knew to be the truth. I kept quiet and he paused for a moment, gazing earnestly at me as though I might have disbelieved him, then said, "Did you know he was thinking of getting engaged to be married?"

I couldn't believe my luck. I had, of course, been intending to raise, in what I hoped would be a subtle manner, the subject of Maria's identity; now the information was being volunteered.

"No," I replied, adding cautiously, "but he did say something about a girlfriend in one of his letters, just a casual reference. Maria somebody or other—I can't remember her surname. In fact, I don't think he ever mentioned it."

40

"Maria Pierides," said Fraser. "She's a schoolteacher here in Limassol."

"Do you know her?"

"Yes. Not well, mind you. I met her a couple of times when we all went swimming together. But Jonathan was always talking about her. He seemed pretty stuck on her and she on him, if the way they looked at each other was anything to go by."

"Do you know where she lives?"

For a moment Fraser looked crestfallen, then a smile warmed his pale features.

"No, I'm afraid I don't. But I know where she teaches. On one occasion we met her outside the school before we all went off to the beach. Why? Do you want to meet her?"

"Yes, I'd like that very much. I'm in the island on business for a spell. I came down from Nicosia today just to see the places Jonathan had told me so much about in his letters. Perhaps you could have a word with her first before you introduce me. The memory of his death may make it too painful for her to talk to me."

"How long will you be here in Limassol?"

"Until Sunday evening."

"Good," said Fraser. "If we get our skates on we can reach the school before she goes home. It's on the outskirts of town. I'll take you there in my jeep."

"That's very good of you."

"Not a bit of it. I'm glad to be of some help. I was afraid at the start that I wasn't going to be able to tell you anything you didn't already know."

"But you have," I said. "And I'm most grateful."

Fraser gave a hesitant smile as he stubbed out his cigarette, then placed his blue beret on his head.

"Come on, sir. It'll be a pleasure to introduce you to Maria Pierides. She's quite a beauty. I said as much to Jonathan on more than one occasion, I can tell you. Your brother had very good taste."

≥ ≥ ≥

The photographs I had seen of Maria Pierides had not lied. She was certainly a beautiful girl. But although her slender, petite figure

41

and classical face were a delight to see, the true measure of her attractiveness lay in the strength of her personality.

At the school, I had stayed in the UN jeep while Fraser had spoken to her. Although he had offered to introduce her to me, she had refused but had instead given him her address, saying that if I stopped by around seven o'clock that evening, she would then be ready to talk to me.

"You see, Mr. Barker," she said, "it was quite a shock to be told this afternoon who you were. I could not have spoken to you then. I needed time to recover—and to think."

"Don't trouble yourself. I understand perfectly. And, by the way, no formality, please. My name is Richard."

She smiled and her eyes grew large, making her face almost childlike in appearance.

"And mine, as you know, is Maria. Now, while I get you a drink, please tell me how you managed to trace me to Limassol. I am very curious."

I began to tell her my story about the photographs and the cards with the Limassol postmark, and she handed me a glass of ouzo, then sat in silence until I had finished. While I sipped the ouzo and felt the warm bite of aniseed in my mouth and throat as I swallowed, she remained quite still, looking at me, her hands clasped together in her lap. For almost a minute we stared at each other in this fashion until she said, "For the past few hours I've regretted agreeing to see you."

"Why?"

She was lifting her glass and it hovered inches from her face as she said, "When I wrote you that letter, I did it to help straighten out my feelings. To close one chapter of my life, so to speak. But it was not long before I discovered I would never be able to forget Jonathan. Perhaps it was only after his death that I realized just how much I loved him. My mind has been in a turmoil again, and when Captain Fraser told me that Jonathan's brother had arrived in Limassol and wanted to meet me, I thought at first it would be a good thing to see you. I thought that somehow it would make me close to Jonathan again. Then, when I got back here to my flat, all my old doubts and fears started haunting me once again. I was sure I had done the wrong thing and that meeting you would only upset me even more. I dreaded the return of the pain and the heartbreak."

"And now? What do you feel now?"

Her gaze was direct, the eyes burning into mine.

"Now my doubts are gone. I felt a deep compulsion to write that letter to you. At the same time I had no wish to reveal my name and where I lived. I was afraid. I am still afraid. But in a strange way, since talking to you the past few minutes I realize it was right to have sent the letter. Now that we have met, I can feel strength returning to me. Instead of a useless despair I can feel determination. It's hard to explain. You must just believe what I say."

I got up and walked across the room to where she sat. I stood directly in front of her and placed my hands on her shoulders. An involuntary tremor ran through her body and she looked up into my face.

"I do believe you," I said. "The fact that you wrote to me, and the very simplicity of the way you put your feelings—how you've expressed them just now—tells me well enough how much you loved my brother. I am in no doubt about that."

She looked at me with an expression of relief in her eyes, and I turned away to stand gazing absently out the window. Her flat was on the fifth floor of a multistory block, and I could see the lights of the town rolling away beneath me. Beyond them were more lights, flashing and twinkling in the gathering darkness as ships entered the harbor or headed out into the open sea. In the room there were only two sounds, the easy rhythm of her breathing and the measured ticking of a clock on a table against the far wall. I turned to look at her again and said, "Now, Maria, tell me about the three men who killed Jonathan—the brothers whom you spoke about in your letter. As much as you know. Every single thing, every minute detail. Where they live, what they look like. Everything."

There was no sign of surprise in either her eyes or her features. She remained impassive, neither distressed nor roused to anger at mention of the brothers. But when she spoke there was a hint of firmness in the tone of her voice.

"Have you come to Cyprus and to Limassol solely to see me? Or have you some other motive in mind? Be honest with me, Richard. Trust me. For Jonathan's sake let us have faith in each other. We owe it to him. We each have our own private grief to bear. We could share it by being utterly frank and open. Believe me, I won't let you down."

I marveled at Maria's shrewdness and inwardly blessed her total acceptance of me. I could see that to achieve success I would need an ally, and what better ally than someone as immersed in the aftermath of the tragedy as she? It was a risk, both for her and for me. In thirty seconds, as I stood looking at her, I decided the issue was important enough for us to share the risk. Somehow, in a strange and chilling way, she seemed able to read my mind, to know what I intended to do even before I was fully certain myself.

I heard myself say, "I want to kill them. I think this has been in my mind since the moment I read your letter. Now that I've met you, I know I'll never be content until those bastards are dead. Murdered. A private vendetta. I need your help."

Without hesitation she replied, calmly and evenly, "You shall have it. I too have wished them dead. Struck down without mercy for what they did. There are times when I wake in the night crying and screaming and I remember. It is all there, fixed in my mind. And I curse them for their inhumanity. Sometimes the nightmare has been so bad that I've lain sweating in the darkness, praying for their death. Mumbling the words aloud so that I could hear them, to give my plea more strength. I used to think, when I was calmer, that this was no more than the ravings of an emotional woman. Now, with your help, I know it can be done. For me it is as if my prayers have been answered. I'll help you, Richard. You'll never regret it."

I murmured my thanks and said, "Then please begin by telling me the names of those men. Who are the brothers?"

"Their name is Tengerakis. Andreas, Nicos, and Stephanides Tengerakis. They are all evil—all brutes. Perhaps the most despicable of the trio is the youngest one, Stephanides. He is the one who boasts of making me his wife."

≥ ≥ ≥

Maria made coffee and for a time would say nothing more about the Tengerakis brothers, but talked quite unconcernedly about her relationship with Jonathan. I sat on the edge of the table in the tiny kitchen while the percolator bubbled, listening intently and answering questions when, from time to time, she would ask about some detail of his early life, of which she knew little.

There was only one moment of sadness. A wistful tone crept into her voice and her eyes seemed to shrink in their sockets as she stared not directly at me but at some point above my head. This came when she explained that Jonathan had hinted he would like her to marry him.

"I asked for more time to think," she said.

Cups and saucers rattled as she placed them on a tray. I could see her right hand trembling a little.

"It wasn't that I didn't love him enough. It was because of what I told you in my letter after his death, this ridiculous business of my father having promised that I would marry Stephanides Tengerakis. It doesn't matter that my father says he does not remember doing anything of the kind. Both my family and the Tengerakis family are traditional Greek Cypriot rural people and still believe in the ritual of tradition. I honestly believe that my father did make a half-hearted offer when he was drunk at some village festival eight years ago, when I was fourteen. Many fathers still pledge their daughters to marriage with some men when the girls are very young. Those fathers have not moved with the times. They see the arrangement as some security for the future. But to me the whole idea of arranged marriage is laughable, as it is to any modern-thinking Cypriot girl."

"But why, if you don't believe in traditions—and I don't blame you for scorning this one—did you not jump at the chance to marry Jonathan, who could remove you from the shackles of the past? After all, you loved him."

"Two reasons. First, although I had repeatedly told my parents before I left home to come here to teach that I would never submit to an arranged marriage, I knew the Tengerakis family was determined to cause trouble for my family. If I had become engaged to a British

45

soldier, then I would have declared myself openly as being against them. I was not too worried about myself, but my mother and father are poor people with a very small farm. The Tengerakis family are perhaps the most powerful people in the district. In every community in Cyprus there is one such family that seems to get what it wants by sheer domination. They could have made life very awkward and difficult for my parents, just as they have done to others throughout the years—to anyone foolish enough to resist them."

She unplugged the percolator and placed it on the tray.

"And the second reason?" I asked.

She smiled. There was a self-conscious gleam in her eyes.

"Simply because no matter how much I might have thought Jonathan was the right man for me, I was not sure I really wanted to be married yet."

"Really?"

She laughed, no doubt because of my incredulous expression.

"Don't look so surprised. I've nothing against marriage. I'm sure it's fine. But I'm young and there are so many things I might want to do with my life before settling down."

"Did you say anything of this to Jonathan?"

Maria shook her head. "No. I did not want to hurt his feelings, and anyway in the long run I might have decided to marry him after all. It wasn't as though he had actually proposed. He was merely testing the ground, so to speak. We used to laugh about his cautious nature. I would sometimes tease him about it. All the same, I did say that I wasn't sure how I would adapt myself to life in England if we got married and lived permanently there. His answer was to invite me to spend his next leave with him on holiday in England."

"Jonathan was always a very practical person," I said.

"Yes. And I'm certain I would have loved the holiday. He was going to take me walking in the woods and lanes of the Hampshire countryside, teach me to ride a horse, drink beer with me in a thatched pub with black beams and roses around the windows. Above all, he wanted me to meet you. I think he was very eager that we should like each other and that you should approve of me. He said he was going to surprise you by writing one day to tell you he was bringing a girl back from Cyprus for a holiday."

"You'd have stayed with my wife and me," I said. "Jonathan's home was always with us after I got married."

"Yes, he told me about that."

"But he never did write," I said. "Why?"

"Because all our plans only started to take shape about two months before he was murdered. I expect he was waiting for the right moment, always hoping I would say yes to marrying him before he said anything to you. Poor Jonathan. He died never knowing my answer."

I remained silent, gazing at her face, softened into sadness by recalling past memories. Reaching out, I touched her arm lightly and smiled so that she might know I understood.

"Come on," I said. "Let's have that coffee. I'll carry the tray into the sitting room. You still haven't told me very much about the men who killed him. Remember, I have plans to make."

"Plans?"

"Yes. Foolproof plans. Plans so well thought out that nothing can make them go wrong. Plans so good that I will be able to commit the perfect murder. Only in this case, not once but three times."

She stared at me for a moment, then said, "*We* have plans to make, Richard. What has to be done must be done by the two of us."

≥ ≥ ≥

Clouds of white dust rose from beneath the wheels of the car as it crunched along a narrow track gouged by bulldozers from a rocky, unfriendly landscape. I closed my side window against the dust now settling in a fine layer over the bodywork and the interior of the car. Immediately I felt the heat mounting in the confined space and a prickle of sweat erupted on my back and chest.

Maria and I had just spent an hour wandering over the site of the ruined city of Curium. Now, in the stifling heat inside the car, I longed again for the freedom and fresh air we had found amid the clusters of pillars and partially excavated buildings. It was a place to excite the imagination, in particular the Temple of Apollo, where in the nineteenth century a hoard of treasure had been unearthed by archaeologists. Closer to the coast lay the restored amphitheatre with

47

its spectacular view of the Mediterranean, while within its precincts exquisite mosaic floors had been cleaned and repaired and brought to life again.

The custodian in his little hut at the entrance gate lifted an arm and waved languidly. I responded with a blast on the horn before turning onto the main road. As I accelerated and changed gear Maria said, "It is stupid for us to go on in this fashion. I must insist that you allow me to accompany you on each occasion. After all, Richard, I am just as involved as you. What's more, I am tired of arguing."

Her face was set with determination. It was plain to see that continued opposition would be useless. We had spent the latter part of the previous evening arguing, and the dispute had flared up again on Saturday morning when we set out to drive to Paphos and up into the Troodos Mountains.

"Last night," she continued, "you asked for my help. I said I would give it. But by helping you I didn't mean just giving you information—that would have been too easy. I meant help in carrying out your plan. Now you talk of the risks involved, the danger to me. I say forget about them. They are not important."

I grunted and opened the side window to allow a welcome rush of cool air into the car. Maria did the same on her side and said, "I am not interested in hearing any more about risks and dangers. I may be a woman, but I know how to look after myself. In Cyprus it is a sensible thing to learn the art of self-defense. If I come with you it will be easier for you because I know these men. I can approach them, talk to them. Heaven knows I'll hate every moment of having to be pleasant to them, but it will be necessary. Despite what they did to me they will never suspect me of actively planning any harm to them."

"Why not?" I asked.

"Because I am a woman, and here in Cyprus women are still expected to be subservient and do nothing for themselves. Besides, they will not know you are Jonathan's brother. You look different, you are much older, and you will be using an assumed name. At least we agreed on that."

I nodded, trying to concentrate on my driving, the passing countryside, and Maria's conversation all at once. I was also still affected by the shock I had received the previous evening when Maria had told me that of the three Tengerakis brothers only one was now living in Cyprus. Stephanides, the youngest of the trio at twenty-two, had gone to work in London, and Nicos, at thirty-one the eldest, to Greece. Only Andreas remained, working as a safety supervisor in one of the island's copper mines and living in the family's farmhouse near the village of Trimithousa. Now I had no choice but to make three separate missions, and to add to my mounting anxiety, Maria had made it clear she would not be thwarted from joining me.

Once again I glanced across at her. She was sitting erect, and her features were stern and unyielding. Then, as we looked at each other, she began to smile and I found myself held by the mixture of womanly guile and charm that has been used for centuries to cajole the unwilling male. I capitulated.

"Very well," I said. "Provided you fully appreciate the dangers involved, I'll say no more and we'll see this through together. Are you afraid?"

Maria remained silent for several seconds. The sound of the engine was obliterated by a roar and an onrush of air as a military vehicle passed us heading for Limassol.

"Yes," she said. "But only now and then. Last night after you'd gone and I had time to think on all we had said, there was a moment when I was very afraid. Afraid for myself and for you too—that either of us might make some mistake and seal the other's fate."

Maria paused to adjust the visor above the windshield and stop the glare against her eyes. When she continued, her face was partially in shadow.

"But then I thought back to the night when the Tengerakis brothers killed Jonathan. They made me stay in the room while they tortured him. They forced me to watch. When I tried to shut my eyes and scream, they forced me to open them, and they held my mouth shut. When I turned my head away they wrenched it back again and twisted my hair so that I had to look to the front and see what they were doing. They took turns holding me, just as they took

49

turns driving poor Jonathan crazy with pain. It was worse than the wildest nightmare. Then they shot him three times, once in the head and twice in the back. Each brother fired one shot. And when I saw the crazed looks on their faces and heard them laughing—evil, demented laughter—I was certain that I too would be murdered. When I think of that night and those hours of degradation and despair, I know quite simply that whatever happens in the future I can never again experience fear as bad as that.''

I felt a great wave of sympathy for her, but when I glanced across and saw the resolute expression of her features as she gazed hypnotically at the landscape, I realized her tremendous reserves of inner strength. In that instant I had no further doubts. She would be a valuable ally and, against those we sought, a formidable opponent.

On rounding a bend I had to swerve to avoid some goats standing in the middle of the road. She laughed aloud as they scattered, bleating and scrambling wildly up the slope, white tails bobbing among the trees.

"Silly creatures," she said. "But quite harmless. What a pity we humans can't be like that."

"Maria," I said. "I want to ask you one more thing about that night. May I?"

She turned her face toward me. The traces of laughter had gone. Her lips were set in a tight line and her eyes were wide as if staring far into the distance.

"Yes. Go ahead. I don't mind, really. Not now. It did me some good to write to you about it. I felt different after that. I feel even better now that I've been able to talk to you—cleansed of the filth perpetrated by those brutes."

"Did Jonathan die quickly?"

I felt Maria move in her seat and looked across in time to see her head nodding. Her eyes were shut. Tears squeezed through between her eyelids and the long, fine eyelashes.

"Yes," she whispered. "I think the first shot killed him outright. He made no sound except for a quick, sharp groan. He was in great pain before Stephanides Tengerakis put the revolver against his head and pulled the trigger. At the moment when Jonathan realized they

50

were going to kill him, he shouted my name. 'Maria,' he called. Just like that. Just once. Then there was nothing in the room but the echo of the shot and the brothers' hysterical laughter. They had tied his hands behind his back and he was lying face down on the floor, quite still. They need not have fired the other two shots, but that is how a ritual killing must be done here in Cyprus. Each member of the gang must have the opportunity to spill the blood of his victim. It is horrible, I know, but it is a fact."

Although deeply shocked by what Maria had just described, I had no wish to remain silent, brooding on my thoughts. I said, "You know, Maria, what we intend to do is in itself a form of ritual murder. We are both driven by the need for revenge. It's a shocking thing to say, I know, but I have no qualms about it. It seems right to me—to kill them because they killed Jonathan."

"Yes, Richard, but there is a difference. When we have killed them, that will be the end of it for us. There will have been some purpose behind our killing. But with the Tengerakis brothers, to kill a person is of no more importance than the killing of a dog, the slaughtering of a sheep or a cow. Before Jonathan they had killed several times, and every time without reason. If they are left unpunished there is no doubt they will kill again. They have always lived by the gun and the knife. The only true justice is that they should die by the same means."

"You are a very determined young woman," I said.

"Perhaps. If I am, it is because in Cyprus determination seems to be bred into our souls. It is a way of life, a part of everyone. It was this streak of stubborn determination that won us our independence; nothing more, nothing less."

I was about to reply when Maria touched me lightly on the arm. In front the road forked. To the left it ran down a slope to the village of Paphos. The Turkish castle was clearly visible and below it the small harbor with its cluster of fishing boats. The red-tiled roofs of the houses glowed in the fierce sunlight, and beyond lay the sea, its calm surface sparkling through a haze of blue.

"We can come back to Paphos," she said. "For now, take the road to the right. In a few miles we will come to the village of

51

Trimithousa and the Tengerakis farmhouse. After that I'll show you the copper mine where Andreas Tengerakis works. It will then be up to us to choose our moment. When do you want to do it?"

"As soon as possible," I replied.

"Good. I too feel this way. We must judge when the time is right—then strike."

Maria's words sent a tremor of nervous anticipation through my body. At the same time I was excited by her decisiveness. When I looked around I saw a sinister gleam in her eyes that did not waver but matched the tone of her voice when she eventually touched the back of my hand, then pointed and said, "Look! Up there on the hill. That is the home of Andreas Tengerakis."

≥ ≥ ≥ **3**

≥ ≥ ≥

Andreas Tengerakis was a superstitious man. He had spent most of the afternoon dozing in the shade of an olive tree. He believed that this, the most sacred tree in Cyprus, had the power to ward off evil spirits. But when he awoke, the nagging feeling of uneasiness was still present, and unknown doubts continued to prey on his mind.

This feeling of apprehension grew stronger each minute, gnawing at his mind because he was unable to attribute his premonition to any particular reason. Indeed, he told himself, there was no reason, no justification for feeling this way. But the doubt persisted and he grew steadily more restless. He lit a cigarette and lay back in the shadowy circle cast by the branches, smoking in quick, nervous bursts. When the cigarette was finished he stubbed it in the dust, shredding the remaining tobacco and paper between his fingers. Then he lit another and sat upright, resting his back against the trunk of the tree.

The smoke curled slowly around his head and drifted away beneath the overhanging branches and out beyond the deep pool of shade. It vanished in a thin, blue stream where the sun beat against the surrounding landscape, turning rocks and dust into an unbroken glare of white. And as Andreas stared, somewhere in the recesses of his mind was the mounting suspicion that somehow this feeling had started with the visit from Maria Pierides.

She had introduced her companion as a Mr. Roberts who was visiting Cyprus to study educational methods and who was interested in geology and wished to visit a copper mine. The man had said something to him about lecturing at a college in England; that an opportunity to see the workings of a copper mine, in particular an ancient mine with shafts dating back to Roman times, would be invaluable both for himself and his students. Maria had added that her headmaster had suggested she help Mr. Roberts with his request.

Andreas had been flattered, although puzzled as to why Maria should have come to him. After all, there were several copper mines being worked in the Troodos region. He had said as much.

"But yours is the oldest," Maria had said. "Everyone knows there is much history attached to it; some fine examples of antiquity are still there to be seen. And anyway you are the only person I know who works in a mine and holds a responsible position. Mr. Roberts has not much time to spend in Cyprus. It would take too long to make a direct approach for permission to the company. You are the supervisor of safety, so you can take whom you please into the caverns and workings."

After a moment's hesitation Andreas had agreed, and they had both smiled at him. This in itself had disturbed him. After the night he and his brothers had killed the young Englishman, Andreas had not even expected Maria to speak to him again, far less smile. But there had been no hint of anything forced in her manner. She had behaved perfectly naturally, as if nothing had happened. It was this controlled composure he found strange and unsettling.

Andreas judged that Maria must have become resigned to her situation. Stephanides seemed determined to marry her not because he loved her but, as far as Andreas could tell, because of some perverse urge. There were times when Andreas did not understand his younger brother. Perhaps, he thought, the stupid girl had seen the error of her ways. Perhaps she realized an honor would be bestowed not only on her but on her family if she married into the most power-

56

ful family in the district. In a way he envied Stephanides. Maria was a beautiful girl and, as she had already shown, not without spirit and pride. There were many times when his thoughts went back to that night in the farmhouse when she had screamed at them and struggled in their arms as they held her, half-clad, her face shining with tears and sweat. Andreas could still smell her animal scent and feel the desperate movements of her lithe, taut body straining against his.

It had been good that night to show who was master, good to see that the power wielded by the Tengerakis family when they worked together, hunting as a team, was still something to be reckoned with. This feeling of domination over others was the greatest satisfaction Andreas knew. In his childhood and youth, this feeling meant a great deal to him. Now, when he was twenty-nine, it still did.

In the mid-sixties, as a teenager, he had played his part in civil disruption in the island. As had so many periods in the history of Cyprus, this had been a violent time. But there had been those within the *Enosis* movement who had felt uneasy about the peculiar ruthlessness of the Tengerakis family, the father and his two sons, Nicos and Andreas. The third son, Stephanides, had been too young to take any active part, although as a schoolboy he had sought information in the marketplaces and other centers where members of the Turkish community gathered and relayed the news to his elders. They planted the bombs, prepared the ambushes, carried out murders on lonely mountain roads and quick, savage hit-and-run attacks in the back streets of Limassol.

Many people had reason to fear the Tengerakis family, and not all were Turks. During the periods of relative peace on the island the Tengerakis family had strengthened its hold on the Greek community of farmers and fruit growers in the district. They had added considerably to their land, not by taking directly but by exerting subtle pressure until eventually the chosen victim was forced to sell to them at a price far below the true market value.

In a number of instances they had encountered resistance. As a result two persons had died and the wife of a vineyard owner had

57

disappeared. The deaths were investigated, but, according to the police, one was evidently a suicide—a farmer found with half his face shot away, a shotgun by his side. The other victim, an elderly woman, had been trapped in her blazing farmhouse. This was officially put down as an accident. On the subject of the missing person the police had made a few desultory inquiries, then gone back to their headquarters in Limassol to add the report to their file marked *Disappearance of Persons*. Not once had anyone hinted to them about the possible involvement of the Tengerakis family; not once, even among the close relatives of the victims, was there a whisper that could throw suspicion on them. The people of the district kept their secrets and suspicions, their fears and mistrust to themselves—an instinct rooted within them through centuries of feudal tradition that in every rural community there must be those such as the Tengerakises who had power and the influence that came with it. What went on in their own district was no concern of outsiders. The people were aware of the evil among them; but there had always been evildoers, and with the simple logic of those whose life was at best a struggle for survival against the elements, they accepted the situation as one that could never change. It was fate.

Andreas Tengerakis was a firm believer in fate, a belief that had helped save his life on several occasions, ingraining upon his mind the need for caution and thoughtful planning no matter what he was undertaking. He recalled with relish how Nicos and Stephanides had left the planning of Jonathan Barker's capture to him. He had made a good job of this, working and reworking every detail so that when the time arrived they carried it off perfectly. They had all agreed it was a master stroke to kidnap the girl with her lover so that she could see for herself what they were going to do.

Andreas ground out the butt of his cigarette and got to his feet. Yes, he had enjoyed himself that night. True, it would have been better if the young Englishman had begged them to stop, asked for their mercy, but his pleasure had been completed by the sight—and the feel—of the girl imploring him to spare her lover's life. He would not forget that night, not for a long time. Never.

When he stepped from the shade of the olive tree he stood for several seconds blinking uncertainly in the strong sunlight. He was meeting them tomorrow afternoon at the mine. Despite the hours of thought he had devoted to the subject since they had called at the farmhouse the previous day, he realized he was still uneasy, perhaps even more apprehensive than before. He walked slowly among the rocks, making his way toward the house.

On the slope to his right were the vineyards, row upon row of gnarled stems and disciplined branches with the grapes, black and green, starting to swell in the constant heat. The vines were heavy this year, laden with clusters of fruit, the promise of a good season. It was satisfying for Andreas to see the acres of vines ripening into wealth and to know he had played a major part in obtaining the land on which the plants now flourished. There was still much more to be achieved, but that would have to wait until Nicos got back from Greece and Stephanides tired of Britain and decided to return.

For the moment, he reasoned, he would do well to concentrate his thoughts on Maria Pierides and the English lecturer. He sensed trouble. It was as well to be prepared.

≥ ≥ ≥

Early in the afternoon Maria and Richard arrived at the copper mine. He parked the car beside a dusty Land Rover that Maria told him belonged to Andreas. The Greek Cypriot stood waiting for them in the doorway of a wooden shed among a cluster of huts and concrete buildings huddled around the headframe of the mine's principal shaft. He shook hands with Richard, smiling broadly and saying, "You are on time, Mr. Roberts. I have heard that the English take pride in their punctuality."

Richard was fully aware of the hint of sarcasm behind the man's words and replied, "We do our best. It's not something you seem to bother with overmuch here in Cyprus."

"You will find if you stay in Cyprus long enough, Mr. Roberts, that we have many strange ways. Strange, that is, to an Englishman."

Andreas turned to Maria, who had moved out of the direct sunlight and into the shade of one of the buildings. She was watching a

59

lizard stalking an insect that had alighted on a broad, flat rock. Andreas came alongside her. His shadow fell across the lizard and the creature vanished, leaving the insect basking in the warmth of the sun.

"You are not teaching today?" Andreas asked.

"No," replied Maria. "I am on holiday. It is the middle of our school term. My headmaster asked me to accompany Mr. Roberts on his visit to the mine."

"You will not be afraid? We will be far underground most of the time. Some of the passages, especially in the old workings, are very narrow and cramped—and unlit. Much of the shoring is crumbling and unsafe. It could be dangerous if you do not take care."

Maria shook her head. Despite her contempt for the man and the tension caused by the thought of what Richard and she intended to do, she made an effort to keep her feelings in check. There was even the trace of a wry smile around her lips.

"I'm aware of the dangers. I'm not afraid. Fear is something that has no real meaning for me now."

She stared directly into his face as she spoke. Andreas could see by the way she held her body that she was tense. His own feelings of unease returned and he tried to determine whether her remark had some underlying significance or was merely defiance. There was, after all, no mistaking the glint of challenge in her eyes.

He glanced toward Richard, but he appeared not to have been listening. He was several paces away, studying the heaps of slag sprawling over the hillside. In the far distance, on either side of the area enclosed by the mine, the pines and cedars of the Troodos forests climbed over and dipped into a series of folds in the mountain range. In the afternoon heat the air appeared to shimmer so that earth, rocks, trees, and sky undulated and rippled in a misty haze of indefinite color. On the lower slopes were flashes of white and pink from flower-laden cistus bushes, but closer at hand across the expanse of the mine the heart had been torn from the side of the hill. Here there were no trees, no bushes, no beauty. As far as the eye could see there was nothing but desolation, a vast area of gray broken only by the towering painted headframes of the various shafts

60

and the untidy mountains of slag where silicate rocks and lava intermingled, sparkling green and red beneath the sun.

Richard was so overwhelmed by the extent of the devastation that he failed to hear Andreas speaking to him. The Greek Cypriot came closer and this time Richard heard the crunch of the gravel beneath the man's boots. He turned around.

"You do not like our mine, Mr. Roberts?" Andreas asked. "I can see by the look on your face that something disturbs you."

"I'm amazed," replied Richard. "Quite simply, it's frightening to see what has happened here. I thought the mine would be completely underground. I didn't expect to see excavating being done on the surface. By the look of things it's laid waste to countless hundreds of acres."

Andreas nodded. "Modern machines bite swiftly, Mr. Roberts, and when they bite they consume much. Here, unlike some other copper mines in the region, we search for ore both above and below ground. But the Romans were the first to develop the industry properly. In Roman times these hills were the richest of all. They had the best ore, and the Romans took it in great quantities. They built galleries far down into the mountain. In some places they managed to reach depths as far down as we have managed to go—six hundred feet, sometimes more. We find their tunnels and galleries everywhere when we blast a new seam. Some say it is like working in a honeycomb down there, the place is so riddled with the Roman workings. Others are more blunt. To them it is like a vast rats' warren."

"It must be difficult work," said Richard. "And highly dangerous."

"It has its dangers. Not all of them are underground. Look up there."

He pointed to a track winding across the face of the hill. A small tractor crawled like a yellow beetle toward the top.

"That's where we are going. Up there—and over the top. That's where the main workings are. Now that will indeed be a sight for you to marvel at. You will know then just how dangerous a mine can be—even above ground. One moment and I will be ready. You may both get into the Land Rover."

61

He hurried off toward one of the huts and disappeared inside. Maria and Richard climbed into the front of the open vehicle. Like the bodywork, the interior was filthy. A cloud of dust rose up as they sat back on the broad bench seat. The upholstery was hot and burned through their clothing. Through the heat came a sickening stench of gas fumes.

Maria looked over her shoulder. There was still no sign of Andreas.

"I'm worried," she said.

Richard glanced at her. She looked extremely nervous. They had talked so much over the weekend about killing Andreas, and in the planning she had shown such a surprising degree of ruthless cunning, that he was now disturbed to see traces of fear and uncertainty creeping into her features.

"Why? Surely he can't suspect anything already?"

"I don't know," she said. "It's purely intuition. He's behaving very strangely. He's being overpolite, almost to the point of sarcasm."

She reached for his left wrist, and her fingers pressed into his skin in a fierce, tight squeeze.

"We must be careful. There are many people working here. You must judge when the moment is right, but remember we have to get away as if nothing had happened."

She released her grip and he said, "I know. It's going to be difficult. Perhaps more difficult than we ever imagined. We may only get one chance. But I'll be ready. I won't make any mistakes."

She smiled nervously. Her eyes were wide, the dark pupils gleaming.

"Are you scared?" he asked.

She nodded.

"I know I said I wouldn't be. But I am. I can't help it."

"I am as well, if that's any help. Unlike our mutual friend Andreas, I've never done anything like this before."

"Don't worry, Richard. By the time we have disposed of Nicos and Stephanides as well, you will have acquired some useful experience."

"Let's get Andreas out of the way first."

≥ ≥ ≥

They heard the door of the hut slam shut and Richard turned his head to see Andreas striding toward the Land Rover. He was whistling and rubbing his hands together. He looked pleased with himself, as if enjoying some private joke. When he heaved his bulk into the vehicle and stretched forward to turn the ignition key, Richard saw that a small hand axe was tucked into the Greek Cypriot's broad leather belt.

The engine throbbed as Richard pointed at the axe and said, "What's that for?"

"Ah, Mr. Roberts." Andreas shouted above the noise of the engine and the grinding of the gears as the vehicle moved slowly up the hill. "That is why I have kept you good people waiting for so long. I couldn't find it in the usual place. Someone must have borrowed it and left it in the wrong spot."

He patted the axe, almost caressing the wooden shaft.

"You see a trusty friend by my side, Mr. Roberts. And you too, Miss Pierides. I have brought him along in case we meet trouble. As I have said, a copper mine can be a dangerous place."

≥ ≥ ≥

They drove to the plateau on the hill, the Land Rover growling in low gear as they negotiated the numerous bends on the narrow track. Once on the top it seemed to Richard and Maria that they were perched on the edge of a monstrous abyss. The peak of the mountain had been blasted away to allow men and machines to excavate a gigantic pit that plunged down in concentric tiers for six or seven hundred feet.

Andreas proudly described the operation. "It has taken us nine years, blasting with ammonium nitrate. We use excavators to pick up the ore. See for yourselves. Down there where the men are working."

They got out of the vehicle and walked cautiously toward the rim. Far below, Richard and Maria could see a number of excavators, long arms clawing and scooping at the base of the abyss. Clustered around them were several dump trucks into which the ore was being

63

emptied. Mounds of pyrite glistened and winked in the sunlight, whereas the base of the pit was like some vast lake, green with layers of copper sulphates. Scores of men, like midgets at this distance, moved unsteadily across the floor of the abyss, while drifting up toward the watching figures came the hum of machinery and the relentless revving of the excavators—giant machines working backward and forward, grinding and groaning, scooping and shoveling, tearing at and destroying the last vestiges of what had once been the side of a mountain.

"Fool's gold," whispered Maria as a dazzling corona of light burst from a truckload of pyrite being driven off toward one of the exits.

Richard smiled and did not speak, but Andreas, who was standing directly behind them, said quietly, "Fool's gold it may be, Miss Pierides, but we have taken almost six million tons of ore from down there. It has helped to make Cyprus wealthy—and it ensures that we stay that way. The Romans themselves took several million tons. It made them very rich."

"Do you think we might see some of the underground workings now?" asked Richard. "It's making me dizzy standing on the edge of this . . . this hole in the ground."

"By all means, Mr. Roberts. There is an entrance to one of the Roman shafts close by. Since you wanted to see the ancient workings, let's approach them by one of their own tunnels."

Andreas walked over to the Land Rover and picked up a safety helmet lying in the rear of the vehicle. Placing it on his head, he tapped the lamp set dead center in the forehead above the brim.

"You'll need these when we go below. The helmets will save your heads from being banged on the rocks, and the light will help you see where to put your feet. Here are two more. Put them on now."

Andreas handed over the helmets, then gestured for Richard and Maria to follow him. He strode across the plateau to a pinnacle of rock jutting above the top of the hill some distance from the edge of the opencast abyss. On the opposite side of the spur the boulder-strewn ground fell away in a gentle slope. In the distance lay a plain

64

with vineyards and fields dotted haphazardly by whitewashed farm buildings and red-tiled houses. Several roads crisscrossed the flat, open expanse like dark ribbons, and far beyond, so indistinct that its blue color wavered and merged with the shimmering haze thrown up by the heat from the land, was the Mediterranean.

They scrambled down the incline for a couple of hundred feet until Andreas signaled a halt beside a curious arrangement of lichen-covered rocks rising vertically from the side of the hill.

"This is it," he said. "We go in now. Switch on your lamps."

The mouth of the shaft was a pool of hostile darkness. Andreas led the way, and within several seconds Richard and Maria found themselves descending an almost vertical flight of steps hewn from the rock. On each side were handholds cut into the rock face, the stone polished to smoothness by grasping fingers over the centuries. After the distant sounds of the machines at work on the floor of the opencast abyss, the silence inside the mine was overpowering. The noise of their feet on the steps rebounded in an echo of vivid clarity, and their breathing, magnified by the rarefied air, became a harsh, animal sound, the more sinister because of the confined space.

A few minutes later the steps in the shaft came to an end. The angle of the slope gradually declined until the ground leveled off in a high, wide gallery. Andreas shined his light on several hewn logs supporting the roof of the chamber.

"The Romans put in these props," he said. He tapped one with his knuckles. "Still as good as new."

A trickle of earth, dislodged by the blow on the log, slithered down the pallid wood. It hissed as it spread out on the floor. Grains of dust danced in the light from their lamps.

"No one has been in this part of the mine for years," said Andreas. "We have never worked it. Too expensive, they say. Anyway, I'm told that the Romans, and the Phoenicians before them, had the pick of the ore. So perhaps it doesn't matter. The main chambers and galleries where our mining is done are about a mile ahead. It's lit there, so it will not be necessary for us to go on groping in the darkness."

For the next hour Andreas led them through a maze of tunnels and galleries which, he explained, like the first one they had entered, had been mined centuries ago. They went up and down ladderways, timbers creaking beneath their weight, and all the while with nothing but the presence of the past and their own gigantic shadows leaping against the rough walls.

Richard and Maria had no opportunity to speak privately, but gradually both began to sense that the killing of Andreas would have to wait. Any attempt would be futile until they returned once again to the gallery beneath the shaft leading out of the mine and onto the hillside. Being underground in strange surroundings gave them a strong feeling of disorientation. The tunnels and chambers, galleries and shafts, especially in the abandoned workings, were so numerous that after a time it became obvious that the farther they went into the heart of the mine, the less likely they were to find a way out by themselves.

In several places their breathing became labored, their lungs gulping ineffectually in the thin air. Once Andreas halted and sniffed the atmosphere, then gestured at them to follow him quickly. Breathing in deep, rasping gasps, they groped their way along the tunnel until they found a shaft offering fresh ventilation. Here, as they stood underneath it, the air came at them in waves, cooling their damp faces and enabling them to breathe normally.

Andreas jabbed a thumb above his head.

"This was not designed for ventilation. They used to take the ore up this way, hauling it in baskets with pulleys and ropes. It's easier now. We have rails, and trucks powered by electricity."

"That air," said Maria, "was foul. You could almost touch it."

Andreas laughed.

"As I say, nothing has been done in this section for many years. Dangerous gases build up that consume what pure air there is. It is possible for anything to happen at any moment down here. We are far underground now."

"You mean an explosion?" asked Maria.

"Yes, Miss Pierides. When copper oxidizes, it creates a high temperature. Sometimes the smallest thing can set it off—a slip of subsiding waste, a man's carelessness—and whoosh, up it goes. You can never tell what might happen."

66

"I think you're trying to frighten us, Mr. Tengerakis," said Richard.

"Frighten you?" There was a brief pause while the Greek Cypriot's hollow laugh echoed around their heads. "Why should I want to frighten you? I cannot think why you should say such a thing, Mr. Roberts. I am merely speaking the truth—stating facts."

Richard ignored this remark. "Isn't it time we were heading back for the top?" he asked.

"Very shortly, yes," replied Andreas. "But we are near to where the mine is now being worked. It would be foolish to go back without seeing that. Come on."

He turned away and the two followed in silence, guided into the oppressive darkness by the blob of light from his lamp. Ten minutes later they stood in a massive chamber several times larger than any they had yet entered. Here and there bulbs suspended on cables slung around the walls close to the roof glowed weakly.

"This is one part where work is now done," said Andreas. "There are several rich seams that come to a point at the end of this gallery. But it is too expensive to keep the labor force fully employed underground. That is why the company switches the workers every other day between here and the opencast site. It is quiet today, with no one around, but tomorrow this place will be so noisy it will be impossible to talk—pneumatic drills, slusher hoists, detonators, trucks rumbling along the rails. Lights on the men's helmets will look like a swarm of fireflies as they hack and chop at the pyrite."

They walked for a short distance through the gallery. A heap of pyrite lying beside a half-filled truck glinted with all the force of gold in the beams from their lamps. For a moment, such was the vastness of the place and so powerful its stillness that Richard had a sudden vision of the past. In his mind's eye he saw not the modern Cypriot miners but the slaves of Roman times, naked and sweating, struggling to carry the jars and baskets of mineral waste and pyrite while their companions, cramped in the narrow depressions in the rock face along which ran the strip of ore, chipped and hacked and breathed in the dust, without rest, without hope. If accidents could happen easily today, what was it like down here, he wondered, for

67

the luckless slaves and the guards and overseers sent to watch over them in Roman times? He had once seen a painting in a New York art gallery of some artist's vision of hell. Now he knew it must have been like that down here in the bowels of the earth.

Andreas broke in on his thoughts. "Come now, we will go back, as you suggested."

During the return journey through the mine the group halted several times, ostensibly for Andreas to point out some feature of the ancient workings. Nevertheless, Richard grew more suspicious as time went past. There was an air of furtiveness in the Greek Cypriot's attitude, as if in some way he was maneuvering them into a situation best suited to his own advantage. On occasions he would simply halt and look back at them, saying nothing; then, having scrutinized them both with the single, baleful beam from the lamp on his helmet, he would turn and plod on.

Richard was also growing more nervous. He would have to act soon if the opportunity was not to be lost. But Andreas soon solved his problem. He halted and gesticulated in the direction of a narrow tunnel running at a right angle away from the main chamber in which they now stood.

"Let me show you this part before we go up. There was once an explosion in here, I believe. The bodies, or what was left of them, were left behind, sealed in by the blast. Now the only life in the place belongs to the rats."

As if to emphasize what he had just said, he bent down and picked up a small rock, then hurled it into the tunnel. It went bouncing and echoing from wall to wall. In the darkness there was a muffled squeak, followed by the sound of scuttling feet. For several seconds the noise made by the stone and the obscene slithering of the rats, sliding and scrabbling into crevices in the walls, filled their ears. Then there was a deep, penetrating silence again such as one feels the moment before a storm breaks.

"I don't want to go in there," Maria said. "I just want to get out into the fresh air and the daylight. I'm tired of having to find my way around in the dark."

The lamp swung around toward Richard and Maria. It was like an enormous, intense eye confronting them.

"You do not like the darkness, Miss Pierides?" asked Andreas.

"No, of course not," replied Maria sharply.

"I do," said Andreas. "I always have. What about you, Mr. Roberts? Are you also afraid of the darkness?"

Richard felt a trickle of sweat in his armpits. Deep inside him, swelling like a knot in the pit of his stomach, was an ache. There was now something deliberately provocative in Andreas's manner. But how could he be certain that Andreas suspected them? Was his attitude of veiled hostility merely his usual behavior? The questions raced in Richard's brain, but despite his mounting anxiety he decided to adopt a show of deference toward his adversary. Perhaps this would provide him with the clue he required.

"Yes," said Richard. "As a matter of fact, I've never liked the dark. Especially in an enclosed space such as this. As a child I was once locked in a cupboard under the stairs in our house. I've never forgotten that."

"Then why did you want to come down into a mine?" asked Andreas. "If I felt as you do, I would stay clear of mines and underground places."

"It's quite simple, really," replied Richard, choosing his words carefully. "I wanted to come down here and, Mr. Tengerakis, I arranged that you would be the person to take me down here, because I have a job to do. When you want very badly to do something, as I do, you're prepared to put up with danger and personal discomfort."

There was a rustling noise above their heads. Andreas looked up at the roof. A colony of bats was hanging from the uneven rock surface. Several had detached themselves from the roof of the gallery and were fluttering wildly, trapped like great black moths in the beam of the light. This gave Richard the opportunity he had wanted. Instinctively he had decided that his nerves could not withstand the strain of any further exploration of the mine as long as he suspected Andreas had some idea of who he was and why he was here with Maria Pierides. In one swift movement he pulled out a thin knife from inside the waistband of his trousers where its bulk had been concealed in a sheath strapped to his thigh.

Andreas swung his light away from the bats. He looked once

69

more toward Maria and Richard. There was muted squeaking as some of the bats, startled by the moving light, bumped against their neighbors in the colony, causing them to fly around the chamber. The sound of their wings was like the sigh of a rising wind.

"A job, Mr. Roberts? What job?"

It had to be now, thought Richard. The Greek Cypriot's lamp was shining fully in his direction. Within seconds Andreas would spot the knife gripped tightly in his right hand. He tried to keep it out of sight against his leg. Four or five yards separated the two men. Maria remained silent, standing to one side, almost touching the wall and close to Andreas. Somewhere in the distance sounded the monotonous plopping of water dripping onto the floor of the gallery from some fissure in the rock.

"My job is to kill you," said Richard slowly and evenly, his voice clear and distinct without a trace of emotion. "For the record, my name is Barker, not Roberts. Do you remember that name, Mr. Tengerakis? I'm sure you do—now."

Almost as he spoke he was bounding toward the Greek Cypriot. There was a blinding glare of light as the beams from their lamps collided. It was like an explosion, but without the noise.

In that instant Andreas lunged sideways and caught hold of Maria. She screamed as her hair was tugged violently, and almost lost her balance. He pulled her backward, toward him, forcing her against his chest and stomach, and twisted both her arms behind her back. With his right hand he pulled the axe from his belt and pressed the flat of the blade against her face.

Somehow, without realizing what he was doing, Richard managed to halt his headlong rush toward the Greek Cypriot, at the same time deflecting the knife away from Maria's body. So great was his confusion that for several seconds his brain could absorb nothing. He was only aware of the sound of his own harsh breathing mingling with Andreas's and a soft whimpering from Maria as the pressure on her twisted arms increased and pain began to flood her body.

Then he heard Andreas say, "Stay where you are, Mr. Barker. If you move again, I will cut her throat."

Andreas released a burst of mocking laughter. "What are you

going to do now, Mr. Barker? Have you the courage to gamble with this whore's life?"

"She's no whore, Tengerakis. In your book anyone who's in love must be a whore. It's the only sort of language you understand."

"Any Cypriot girl who takes an English soldier for a lover must be a whore. I see it no other way. Your pretty English boy of a brother was killed because he dared to take the woman promised my youngest brother. If she was not a whore when this happened, your brother made her one. He was executed for that reason and also because he was unlucky enough to be a British soldier. Like so many Greek Cypriots, I hate British soldiers—hate them for what they did to us when we wanted our freedom."

At once Richard felt the hatred he had nurtured for so long take possession of him. It was a force he was powerless to halt. The utter contempt, the disgust, the sheer loathing he felt for this man, for his beliefs, and for what he had done to Jonathan, rose like a surge of bile in his throat. His palm around the handle of the knife was slippery with sweat and his hand shook, but blind anger sent him forward, mindless of Maria's safety.

Richard's sudden, abrupt lunge forward and upward took Andreas totally by surprise. The knife slashed his right arm. The axe fell from his fingers, thumping across the toe of his boot, then went skidding along the floor of the gallery. As Andreas released a roar of pain, Maria felt his hold loosening. She jerked one of her heels against his shins and wriggled her body. Although her arms felt limp and numb, she was able to drag them away from the Greek Cypriot's weakened grip. She tottered forward several paces, then tripped and fell headlong, the light from her lamp going out as the helmet banged against the wall.

Richard was thrusting with the knife once again when Andreas threw the switch on the side of his helmet and extinguished the lamp. At the same time he stepped to one side and threw a punch that connected with Richard's midriff. Richard staggered sideways, colliding with the wall, then, feeling an onrush of air as the Greek Cypriot lunged at him, he lowered his head and flung himself against the man's stomach. Their bodies collided. There was a crack

71

like a pistol shot as his helmet struck the buckle on the Greek Cypriot's belt. Andreas felt the breath forced from his body. Beneath his rib cage came wave after wave of surging pain. For an instant he stood quite still before falling backward. Then he saw Richard's upraised arm with the knife blade curving in toward his chest. Instinctively he grabbed at the Englishman's wrist and, as his fingers closed around it, toppled back to bring Richard crashing on top of him.

When the Greek Cypriot's head struck the wall, the blow loosened his helmet. It slipped to one side, then fell off. For several seconds both men were dazed by the swiftness of the struggle and the force of their bodies smacking against the rock. Andreas still held Richard's wrist and had twisted it around so that the knife blade pointed back toward the Englishman. Richard raised himself to his knees and quickly dropped to one side so that the Greek Cypriot could not knee him in the groin. He tried to force his wrist against the pressure exerted by Andreas and for a moment thought the man was weakening. But the moment was all Andreas needed to raise himself slightly and bring his other arm up from his side. His hand locked around Richard's free wrist. Now they were like two wrestlers locked in combat at arm's length, both trapped in a hold that could be broken only by one destroying the other's strength.

Slowly Richard was edged backward. At first the light from his lamp had shone fully on the Greek Cypriot's face. He had seen the sweat-lined features, the mouth and eyes distorted with a mixture of pain and hatred. Now, as Andreas's superior strength began to tell, the light slipped away from his face and up across the wall, where it remained motionless, like a round, yellow circle, suspended in space.

Richard's wrists were aching. His fingers still gripped the knife, but he knew it was useless now. The blade continued to point directly at his own chest, the wrist snapped fully back, numbed by the pressure of the Greek Cypriot's fingers. The two men panted and heaved. Gradually Richard became aware that his strength was ebbing. The knowledge made him try more desperately than ever to resist. He attempted to drag Andreas toward him so that he could kick him. But the Greek Cypriot sensed the move in advance and stood his ground. At the same time, he spat in the Englishman's face.

The spit struck Richard on the nose, and in that instant his last reserve of strength was broken. It drained from him like the emptying of a dam. And when it was gone, the knife was at his feet. He was being propelled backward, faster and faster, until with a sickening lurch he was hurled against the wall and the Greek Cypriot was pressing against him, both hands around his throat, the thumbs gouging the underside of his jaw, pushing his neck upward and back. Richard's head was banged against the rock, the noise made by the metal helmet filling his ears. Andreas pushed and mauled and tore at him in all the frenzy of madness. Richard sensed the rotten stench of his opponent's breath against his face. He was like a puppet, feeling it all happening to him, too weak to fight back.

Although Richard's eyes were glazed over with pain as he slowly lost consciousness, he was sufficiently aware of the bobbing light from his lamp to see a shadow rise like a scepter alongside and almost behing the Greek Cypriot. Maria's scream rang bell-like in the gallery as her upraised arms came down. At that moment Richard felt the hands go from his throat. Andreas bellowed as a short, sharp sound, like the cracking of a seasoned piece of timber, burst on Richard's ears. Then the Greek Cypriot was staggering past him, howling so that the cavern was filled with the echoes battering on each other—a hideous cacophony, full of evil, hopeless with despair. Several times Andreas blundered against the wall before he slid, face bumping on the hewn rock, and pitched full length along the floor.

For several seconds the echoing cries rang on in the chamber, rising and fading until they died among the maze of tunnels leading away from the main gallery. There was silence again, except for the rasping sound of Richard's breathing and the rustling of the bats in the roof directly above his head.

Richard felt Maria's arms around him and her body, trembling like his, pressed against his side. He stroked her hair and held her face against his shoulder. Minutes passed and they said nothing to each other, not even when Richard found the strength to leave the

73

wall and looked down to see the axe, its blade embedded halfway to the shaft in the Greek Cypriot's skull.

≥ ≥ ≥

After the shock receded, they dragged the body into one of the narrow side tunnels, obviously long unused, to judge from the amount of rubble strewn in heaps along the floor. Twenty yards in from the gallery the tunnel had been sealed by a fall of rocks. They wedged the body against the pile, then started to cover it with boulders and slabs of stone. There was dust and grime and the close confines of the tunnel made them sweat profusely, but they labored without a word. Within half an hour the job was completed. Andreas Tengerakis was in his grave, buried under what appeared to be a massive extension of the rock fall blocking the tunnel.

Some distance away, under a smaller pile of rocks, Richard concealed the axe and the Greek Cypriot's safety helmet. For some reason he found handling the axe more distasteful than touching the body. The extent of Maria's hatred was there for him to see when he tried to dislodge the axe. At one point he almost gave up in his attempts to remove it. Then somehow it was free and he forced back the vomit rising in his throat.

Hand in hand the pair made their way along the gallery toward the flight of steps, stopping for several minutes to retrieve Richard's missing knife. Wearily they climbed toward the circle of light at the mouth of the shaft. Once in the open they stood for a time gulping at the clean, pure air. It was quiet and the noise of men and machinery had gone from the bottom of the opencast workings away to their right. It was early evening and the sun was sinking behind the forests capping the ridges of the Troodos Mountains. There were streaks of red in the sky and the sun burned like a bloodshot eye. Against the gray and blue and wisps of red were the silhouettes of griffon vultures wheeling and dipping, crying into the rising wind.

"What about the Land Rover?" Maria asked.

Richard glanced up toward the vehicle. A plan formed quickly in his mind; it was worth taking a chance. He took hold of Maria's arm and propelled her up the final part of the slope onto the plateau. They climbed inside the Land Rover and he started the engine.

He had never driven one before, but it did not matter. It was downhill all the way toward the cluster of huts. Their luck held. There was no one there. The place, unlit and silent, looked deserted. He parked the vehicle behind a shed. They got out and walked slowly toward their own car. Every second they expected to be challenged, to hear a voice calling to them from out of the twilight. But no one spoke, and they drove away unnoticed, down the dusty track and out onto the main highway.

Ninety minutes later they were seated in Maria's Limassol flat. They had washed the grime and sweat from their bodies. Each was satisfied, flushed with success. The horror of the struggle in the mine was starting to fade. They were cool and relaxed. Maria switched on the radio.

A man's voice, tinged with hysteria, was talking of rioting in Nicosia, then announced that a coup had taken place. The president, Archbishop Makarios, had been assassinated in the ruins of his bombed palace.

≫≫≫ **4**

≥ ≥ ≥

Later we discovered that the archbishop had survived the attack on his palace and had managed to flee to Paphos, from where, eventually, he was taken by helicopter to the British Sovereign Base at Akrotiri and then on to make an appearance before the United Nations in New York. But for several hours all we knew was what we heard from the garbled radio reports, which said Makarios was dead and Nicos Sampson had taken his place as president.

The question uppermost in our minds, and indeed in the minds of everyone in Cyprus, was whether the Turkish government in Ankara would order an invasion of the island as a result of this situation, which had been engineered by the Greek colonels in Athens. As we now know, it took some time for this action to materialize, but in the hours after first hearing of the crisis Maria and I were convinced that at any minute Cyprus could become a battleground.

It was a chance remark of Maria's—that in the general confusion and disruption taking hold of the island little notice would be taken of the disappearance of one individual, Andreas Tengerakis—that clinched the idea slowly formulating in my mind. As I look back on it now, it was a mad, dangerous scheme, an act of folly that was instrumental in placing me in my present predicament. If only I had listened to the voice of caution! But at that time there was little sanity in me, only an overwhelming desire to kill twice more so that Jonathan might be avenged and to finish the job as quickly as possible.

"You're right," I said to Maria. "Therefore, in the present circumstances if we were to leave the island for a few days, no one would miss us. You're on holiday; I can do as I please."

Maria poured coffee and placed the pot on the table. As she handed me a cup there was a mischievous gleam in her wide, expressive eyes.

"What are you suggesting, Richard?"

"That we go to Greece. Right now. Today. You argued long enough to persuade me to let you accompany me, so what about making the journey now? We were successful in disposing of Andreas Tengerakis. While luck is with us let's go for Nicos. Then I can get back to England and finish the job in London. Finis."

"We would never get a flight out of Nicosia. The airport is closed now because of the fighting."

"Oh, Lord, I hadn't thought of that. Not much of a mastermind, am I?"

Maria sat down alongside me. She was smiling, no doubt, I presumed, because of my misguided enthusiasm. I should have known the true meaning behind that smile. After all, we had spent enough time in each other's company. Later, I realized she had smiled in that way because she too had been thinking of going to Greece; only her thoughts could be translated into action, thanks to her shrewdness and knowledge of the area.

"There is another way besides flying to get to Greece," she said. "By sea. And"—she raised her eyebrows and at the same time twitched her nose—"as it happens, I know a freighter captain who makes a regular run. What is more important from our point of view, his ship goes to Volos. Nicos Tengerakis works in Volos. At least for some of the time. He drives a taxi and lives no more than twenty miles from there. The Tengerakises have relatives in Greece. Nicos works for them—and as far as I know lives with them—in Makrinitsá, a village in the Pelion Mountains."

I tried to picture a map of Greece in my mind. I had been to Athens on business several times, but of the rest of the country I knew little or nothing.

"Where's Volos?"

"North of Athens. About two hundred miles farther north. It is a busy seaport, ships coming and going all the time. In fact, Richard, because there are so many crews of ships going ashore into the town, it is the ideal place for us. As it is, we would not have much time there."

"How long?"

"Less than twenty-four hours. My friend's ship leaves Limassol on a Tuesday and gets to Volos in the early hours on Friday morning. The men load and unload throughout the day and sail again late Friday evening, arriving back here in Limassol on Monday. The ship makes the journey every fortnight."

"I expect you're telling me all this in such detail because tomorrow is Tuesday and you already know that this particular Tuesday is a sailing day."

Maria made no attempt to disguise her shrewd smile. "How ever did you guess, Richard?"

"Because you are a determined young woman, Maria Pierides. Both determined and cunning."

"I thought you liked determination in a person."

"Oh, I do. Believe me, I do. However, my girl, no amount of determination is going to get us over the fact that although I have a passport, it does not contain an entry visa for Greece. What about you?"

"Exactly the same," she said. "But there is no need to worry. We shall not require them."

"Don't be ridiculous. Everyone needs a passport to land in a foreign country—and visas and things. It's all highly controlled. Bureaucracy sees to that."

She shook her head. Once again her eyes were shining with restrained mirth.

"Not everybody. You and I can dispense with the usual formalities. I should know. I've done it before."

81

"How, for goodness' sake?"

"We sign on as ship's crew. This means we can land in Greece for a brief visit. We need our passports, of course, but no visas. Have you got your passport with you?"

I nodded.

"Good," she said. "Then let me have it now and the captain of the ship will arrange everything for us."

"You said just now you'd done this before. When?"

"I went to Greece on the same ship with Jonathan not long before he was murdered. I had only a week's holiday at the time. He very much wanted to see Greece, even though it was only for such a short time. But we both loved ships and the sea. And besides setting foot in Greece there was the opportunity to see so many of the Greek islands as we sailed to and from Volos. It was a happy time. Despite everything that has happened since then, I still remember that week as one of the happiest of my life. If it taught me anything at all, it was that he loved me far more than perhaps I realized."

I did not reply but just sat watching her, seeing the mood of her face changing with the tone of her voice, a distant, almost vague expression creeping into her eyes. Perhaps if I had been more alert I would have grasped there and then the clue she had unwittingly placed before me that Jonathan's death had come shortly after their trip to Greece. Somehow I should have appreciated the connection between that ship and his murder, realized the possibility that aboard a vessel sailing out of Limassol there could well be a person who had links with the Tengerakis family.

Of course, I went ahead suspecting nothing of this. Even now I'm not absolutely certain that the *Fontana Amorosa* was the one flaw in what I had assumed were foolproof plans. But, eventually, when the time came and I knew something had gone wrong—dreadfully wrong—and I was forced through worry and confusion to cast my mind into the past, searching for answers, the voyage to Greece aboard the *Fontana Amorosa* kept on recurring. All the same, by then it was too late to alter the course of events.

I tried to telephone Christos Charalambous at his office in Nicosia, but he was not there. I left a message with a secretary, asking her to tell him that in view of the present mood of unrest on the island I was going to take advantage of an offer made by some friends to go cruising for several days, perhaps a week, in the Mediterranean. He was not to worry about me. I was sorry that under the circumstances I would not be able to attend his nephew's wedding. I was certain he would understand.

I felt especially bad about this particular aspect of my deceit, but the secretary assuaged a little of my guilt by replying that because of the political upheaval she doubted if the wedding would now take place on schedule. I then asked her to cable my wife in England telling her I was safe and well, thanked her, and rang off.

≥ ≥ ≥

The *Fontana Amorosa* had a beautiful name, but by no stretch of the imagination could she be called a beautiful ship. At one time she had been painted white with a funnel of vivid blue, but years of neglect had rendered her dowdy and unkempt, with the faded paintwork blistering and peeling and the rust showing red in dark blotches on her plates. The bridge was in the bows and she looked top-heavy, but, surprisingly, after we had put to sea and the waves came at us with ever-increasing strength, there was no wallowing, no slithering, sliding motion from side to side, then up and down, to tear your guts apart; there were merely a mild tremor as her bows met the swell and the controlled motion of her power as she rose and fell gently, cleaving on toward Volos with her cargo of timber.

Her captain was a swarthy, rotund Greek Cypriot called Stavros, one minute smiling and laughing, his great belly wobbling as if about to spill from the waistband of his baggy trousers, the next minute pacing the deck shouting abuse at some member of the crew, his face stern and unforgiving. However, despite his bouts of unpredictable and highly temperamental behavior—perhaps even because of them—the crew appeared to like and respect him.

At around fifteen hundred tons the *Fontana Amorosa* did not carry a large crew: three officers and fourteen seamen, ranging from a handsome youth of sixteen or seventeen, always whistling or singing romantic songs almost mournful in their ecstasy, to an old man

83

who on every occasion I happened to see him was carrying buckets of swill from the galley to tip them over the side.

Captain Stavros made me very welcome. I never found out what Maria had told him about us and why we wanted to take this rather hurried voyage aboard his ship. He seemed to accept it as perfectly normal that she should turn up at the last minute requesting a passage under our unorthodox pretext of being supernumerary members of his crew. Nor did he make any comment about my surname being the same as Jonathan's or that earlier in the year she had made the voyage under similar circumstances accompanied by another man. Apparently to Captain Stavros no foible of human nature seemed extraordinary.

He attached a piece of paper bearing his florid signature to each of our passports. This stated that for the purposes of this particular voyage to and from Greece we were additional members of his crew and subject to his discipline and command. A spare cabin with two bunk beds was miraculously cleaned up and dusted within an hour of our arrival on board. We ate at his table in the cramped mess, had the complete run of the ship, and in the evenings either accompanied him up on the bridge or sat in his cabin, often with one of the other officers. There we drank wine and talked while in the background the music of Theodorakis pulsated from a battered portable phonograph.

Sometimes a surfeit of wine and heady, emotional music would send Captain Stavros into a sentimental mood, reminiscing about his youth and the voyages he had made. Now and then he would weep as the shimmering chords of the bouzouki mingled with the voice of the singer, reducing us all to silence with the haunting, almost mystical sound.

Once he said to me, "When I am in port at Volos I cannot play this music. It is considered by the Greek authorities to be revolutionary and is therefore banned. I tried it once and was reported. The police came on board. I ordered them off, saying, 'This is my ship. I am captain, and I do as I please aboard my own ship.' Eventually they went, threatening me they would return with the military. They never did. But since then I have been careful. I have never played the music of Theodorakis again while in port. I have no wish to be fighting people. I like to be left alone in peace. So I play the records only when we are at sea. At least here I am free from interference and the bigoted stupidity of narrow minds."

"The colonels won't rule Greece forever," I said. "After they go, you can play your music whenever you like."

He looked at me intently, a wistful expression in his sad, brown eyes.

"You are right. They may find themselves out of favor before very much longer after the tragedy that has befallen Cyprus. But what good will it do? One country will be freed from tyranny, another will just begin to feel the rule of a ruthless dictator."

"You mean Cyprus could go the same way?" I asked.

He shrugged his shoulders but remained silent. The music had finished. The needle clicked monotonously as the turntable continued to spin. Maria rose and turned the record over. There was a hiss as the needle scraped on the edge, then a fast, hypnotic rhythm began to dominate all other sounds in the cabin. Maria stood in the center of the floor, clapping her hands in time to the music, laughing and swaying.

"Come, you two, join in the fun," she shouted. "Politics makes me sad. Why is it that men must always talk politics and make me unhappy?"

Captain Stavros winked at me, then leaned forward and squeezed my arm. "She is a wise girl, Mr. Barker. Good girls are precious, but there are many of them. Wise girls are rare. You must look after her."

All at once the three of us were singing and clapping, the beat of the music thumping in our ears, while beneath our stamping feet the *Fontana Amorosa* dipped and rose, shivering a little like some nervous animal, trembling in the Aegean Sea, bows pointing toward the Gulf of Volos.

≥ ≥ ≥

At first it was slightly embarrassing that Captain Stavros assumed Maria and I were lovers. In his and the crew's company, however,

85

we began to appreciate the joke, and there were even moments when, by a gesture or a touch of mutual affection, we played the role that was expected of us. But in private, behind the door of the tiny cabin, the situation was fraught with difficulty and numerous minor irritations which, if not kept in check, were likely to fray tempers and blight an otherwise uncomplicated relationship.

On the first night aboard we agreed to undress in the dark, banging shins and elbows on every imaginable projecting surface in the cabin. On the second night the light was left on while I showered and Maria got ready for bed alone. When I returned she was already in the bottom bunk, face turned toward the bulkhead. The shower compartment was so cramped it was impossible to dry oneself there, so I unwrapped the towel from around my waist and dried my body in the cabin with the light on, only a couple of feet from where she lay. When I switched off the light and clambered inexpertly up to the top bunk she said good night and I heard a movement as she turned, making herself more comfortable for sleep. It may have been my imagination, but I thought I heard her sigh a deep, long sigh. The sound stayed in my head for some time as I lay in the darkness listening to Maria's rhythmic breathing and the throb of the *Fontana Amorosa*'s engines far below deck.

On Thursday, the third night out of Limassol, we went to the cabin earlier than usual. The ship was due to dock at Volos at five o'clock the following morning. Maria and I wanted to be fit and rested for the long, uncertain day ahead. As it happened we had both drunk too much of the captain's wine, a blood-red concoction that he lovingly referred to as "the red infuriator." When I returned from my ritual shower I found, to my surprise, that Maria had not yet got into bed. Instead, she was seated on the edge of the bunk, absolutely naked.

I think that for several seconds I just stood with the door half-open staring at her. Despite the harsh glare of the electric light bulb, with its cracked white plastic shade, and the faded green paint on the bulkheads, she radiated beauty amid the ugliness of neglect. The light fell across her dusky skin so that her small, neat body appeared to glow, soft and vulnerable. She was stretching back her shoulders,

86

hands on a level with her head, mouth open, yawning. She looked across at me, startled for a moment by my abrupt opening of the door. Then she smiled and allowed her hands to drop back onto her knees. I started to mutter an apology and was about to close the door again when she got to her feet and took hold of my right hand.

"Come in, Richard. Let's stop fooling ourselves."

That was all she said. I stepped into the cabin and shut the door. I could use all the usual excuses for what happened between us; I could even invent more. I could say we were tense and nervous about the mission we had undertaken to carry out in Greece, each apprehensive for our own and the other's safety. I could pretend that the danger we had already been through together, resulting in our enforced proximity, sent us into each other's arms for mutual comfort and affection. It would be quite false to pretend or invent. We were, quite simply, man and woman, and the needs within us were strong, demanding satisfaction and release.

We took pleasure from each other's bodies from the moment they touched, mine still wet and slippery from the shower, hers warm and pliable, small breasts rubbing against my skin, my hands intertwined with hers, fumbling with the towel around my waist until it slipped away and fell across my toes. I think it was at that stage that I appreciated how small she really was. Her hair was tickling my chest and I laughed and ran my hands along her sides, up across her shoulders to take hold of her head. She wriggled against me, then I bent my head and turned her face up to meet mine. We kissed with a ferocity that made us both gasp, and for a fleeting moment I wondered whether in her imagination she was really kissing Jonathan and not his elder brother. Any last flickering doubts that by making love to Maria I was manufacturing a situation that could only succeed in complicating both our lives were dispelled when I cracked my head against the side of the top bunk while trying to lift her onto the lower bed.

I swore and almost dropped her, and she clung to my waist, laughing uncontrollably. I rubbed my temple, then as the pain eased I too began to laugh. Suddenly I was aware of the hilarity of trying to make love in a squashed-up cabin where the bunks were so close

87

together, one on top of the other, that conventional positions were impossible—as were most other methods, for that matter.

We were both laughing, kneeling face to face on the floor. Had Captain Stavros passed our cabin at that moment I'm sure he would have approved of, perhaps even envied, the sound of our carefree behavior. I dragged a mattress down beside us and we rolled onto it and lay on our sides, pressed hard against each other. When eventually she lay on her back beneath me and I ran my hands over her body, cupping her breasts in my palms, she looked so delicate, so childlike, that I grew even more amazed at her inner strength and determination, the courage hidden beneath the innocent appearance and feminine beauty. She gave herself to me without inhibition and I responded, so that when our release came we cried out in unison. The sound seemed to echo around the bulkheads long after the moment had passed, and when I opened my eyes she was smiling.

Already the first hints of laughter were rising in her throat. I raised my eyebrows and she said, "Who would have thought that only two nights ago we were undressing in the dark?"

I hugged her against me and kissed the lobe of her right ear. She ran a finger along my spine, then started to make small circles on my back. Life felt good. Despite the steel floor beneath the thin mattress and the glare of the overhead light I felt comfortable, deeply satisfied, as if somehow I had no cares in the world, no worries, no hate, and tomorrow was not tomorrow but some day in the distant future that might never happen. Maria seemed to feel the same way as she lay against me, eyelids drooping. Our arms encircled each other. The touch of her breath was soft on my cheek, and underneath our bodies the ship rolled gently, with now and then a shudder along the deck.

We awoke almost simultaneously. The light from the bulb blinded us, and we tried to shield our eyes from the yellow glare. The ship had stopped, and outside the cabin porthole sounded a clash of gears, then the protesting noise of an engine under strain. Men shouted and several tremors ran through the vessel as if heavy weights had been dropped onto the deck. My shoulders and back were aching as I rose to make my way to the porthole. I peered through the glass, screwing up my eyes against the pure light of early morning.

The *Fontana Amorosa* was tied up alongside a quay. A crowd of men were gathered on the dock beside her berth waiting for unloading of the cargo to get under way. There were several trucks and a couple of fork-lifts.

"Hey, we're here," I said to Maria. "We're in Volos."

She looked around her, at the drab surroundings and the mattress with its tousled sheet strewn on the floor. She raised herself slowly onto her knees, then gave a warm, spontaneous burst of laughter that made me forget for the moment my throbbing head and stiff back. I too started to chuckle.

"All this," she said, throwing wide her arms to encompass the untidy floor, herself, and my own weary figure beside the porthole, "all this is what comes of not undressing in the dark."

≫≫≫ **5**

≥ ≥ ≥

Nicos Tengerakis had spent several weeks in eager anticipation of the wedding in Makrinitsá. The celebrations would last one week, and he stood to make plenty of money.

It had been a shrewd move on his part when, earlier in the year, he had written to his cousin in Greece to offer his services to run the only taxi service in the mountain village. His cousin was frequently in poor health and, having lost much money, had thought of selling his business. But Nicos, always alive to the possibility of making a small fortune, had said he would help to put things back on a proper footing. So far, his efforts were succeeding.

There was a bus service between the village and the town of Volos, but many people, regardless of wealth and personal status, used taxis. They were reasonably cheap and offered more comfort than a journey in a crowded bus with people and possessions crammed together in the heat and dust, surrounded by the sweet smell of diesel oil. Since the majority of people used public transport of one kind or another, there was a good living to be made as a taxi driver.

Nicos and his cousin had two taxis, a blue Ford and a large black Mercedes-Benz heavy with chromium plating. Nicos drove the

Mercedes, because it was big and gleaming; it made him feel good to sit behind the steering wheel and feel the power flowing from the engine.

In a way, in this week of the wedding Nicos was especially lucky. His cousin had taken his wife and two children away on holiday to visit relatives in Corinth. This had been arranged much earlier in the year before news of the wedding was announced, and Nicos was on his own. Of course it meant more work for him, but in turn there would be a great deal more money in his pocket. His arrangement with his cousin guaranteed him a percentage of his own takings in addition to his usual weekly wage. His cousin had told him before going on holiday that if he was too busy he could enlist the aid of Alexis Savides, another Makrinitsá villager, to drive the Ford. But as the week progressed, Nicos took pleasure in coping with the extra demand for his taxi, juggling with times when fixed appointments threatened to clash, driving the casual trade at unsafe speeds up the winding mountain road between Volos and Makrinitsá and back, working at all times of the day and night, refusing no one, the sound of his clicking meter sweet music to his ears.

Now, by Friday morning, with three full days of festivities to go, Nicos had already taken in a great deal of money. In the remaining days he stood to make as much again. He was happy; he enjoyed his work. Above all, he enjoyed making money.

It was also good to be away from Cyprus for a time, freed from the constant pressure of being one of the Tengerakis family with a dubious reputation to maintain in his home village. There had been moments, all the same, since he had first heard the news on the radio of the coup in Cyprus, when he had wanted to return, to go back and fight to ensure the success of the revolution he had always hoped would come one day. This he would certainly do if ever Turkey invaded the island, and to judge by the latest news, it would not be long before such a thing happened. It could happen any day. Nicos wanted it to happen. His hatred for the island's Turkish community was even greater than the contempt and loathing he had for the British.

But for the moment, with his cousin away and the people flocking

94

to and from Makrinitsá because of the wedding celebrations, thoughts and dreams of being at home in Cyprus at the center of the fighting were suppressed. In his mind he had only one vision, and that was of his pockets growing heavy with money.

≥ ≥ ≥

As Nicos made his first journey on Friday toward Volos, the early morning sun bathed Mount Pelion in a soft, iridescent light. The winding road from Makrinitsá plunged from the rock-strewn landscape of the heights of the mountain range through olive groves and orchards of peach and apple, at times threading leisurely among forests of chestnut and plane trees. The mountainside was pockmarked with wooded valleys falling almost vertically from the edge of the road. In other places, great outcroppings of rock hung on one side or the other, the roadway separated from oblivion only by low stone walls alive with the reds, yellows, and blues of the flowers of creeping plants. There were fast, straight stretches followed by tight, narrow bends where on one side the woods climbed steeply away out of reach and on the other the tops of the trees were clearly visible in the next valley far below. The sun shone through the branches of the trees, the muted colors glowing in a patchwork of semitransparent brilliance, broken here and there by streaks of glaring white from houses scattered almost secretively on the side of the mountain.

Visible from many stretches of the road was the Gulf of Volos. This morning the surface of the sea was like some vast inland lake, flat calm and unruffled. Now and then shafts of sunlight burst skyward, reflected from the hulls of passing vessels so that the sea appeared to glitter in anticipation of the heat to come. In the shade of the trees on the mountainside it was still cool, and close to the banks of the numerous streams pockets of mist hung suspended like wreaths of smoke among the branches.

With the side windows of the Mercedes open to their limits the interior of the taxi was fresh and comfortable. Nicos enjoyed himself accelerating fiercely on the straight stretches of roadway, then braking to ease the heavy car around the twisting bends. There was a

95

warm glow in the pit of his stomach from the jug of coffee he had drunk before leaving. His fingers drummed aimlessly on the polished rim of the steering wheel.

Nicos Tengerakis felt content and at peace with the world. In his mind remained vivid images of the hour he had spent late the previous night with one of the wedding guests. He wanted to see her again. That hour had been good. He had said so after they had coupled in the back of the taxi, parked without lights in a clump of olive trees close to the road. She would not commit herself. But she was a young girl, not long out of her teens, and Nicos knew well by now that such girls always responded in the same way. Like the others, she would be back.

Nicos liked the young girls best of all, the tall ones with their long, smooth legs and their breasts newly formed to maturity so that cupped in his hands they felt firm and smooth. He liked to excite the girls by running his palms over their flat, trembling stomachs, feeling beneath his fingers the measure of his roughness and power and the depth of their submission. He whistled between his teeth as he thought again of last night. Yes, she would be back for more just like all the others. He knew how to handle young women; he had plenty to teach them, things they could never learn from youths their own age, who were often every bit as raw as themselves. They could see he was a man of the world. That was why they always made some excuse to meet him again, although immediately after the first time they tried to act nonchalant.

A rush of air rocked the Mercedes slightly as a bus went past toward Makrinitsá. Nicos steadied the steering wheel, then swerved at a bend to avoid an old woman crossing the road. She was bent beneath the weight of a basket fastened across her back and pulling on a rope attached to a donkey. The animal had two large panniers on either side of its body. When the woman saw the car she turned and yelled in the donkey's face, at the same time tugging hard on the rope. Nicos blew his horn and cut in behind the animal. The noise and the roar of the engine sent the donkey bounding forward, knocking the old woman to one side. Some fruit spilled from her basket, bursting and rolling across the roadway. Nicos laughed. In his

96

rear-view mirror he could see the woman shaking both fists in the air.

With the road clear once more his thoughts returned to the girl of the night before and to previous encounters. There was one thing he dearly wanted to repeat again. One girl was good, but two at the same time—now that was something. It had happened once in Cyprus. Walking along a beach, he had come across two teenage girls sunbathing on rocks in a sheltered cove. He had watched for some time as they lay side by side in the sun and first one, then the other, removed her swimming costume, giggling together at their daring; then they stretched out naked in the heat.

At first, when Nicos had walked toward them, they had jumped up, embarrassed and angry at his laughter, but they were young and naive and he knew it. He used words to charm them, complimenting them both on their beauty, the flattery oozing from his lips. He could see the girls starting to enjoy it, reveling in the new experience, excited by it, gradually flaunting themselves as innuendo and teasing comments flowed from them in response.

He had stripped off his own clothes and swum naked with them, the trio playing like porpoises in the water, each girl making a play for his body. Later, on the sand in the shadow of a high gray cliff he had taken them both, the novel experience heightening his pleasure and the girls' to such a degree that they had lain and moved in a tangle of limbs for what seemed like hours.

Of course he had known at the start they were British, and later they told him they were school friends out from England for their summer holiday. This in itself had added an extra thrill, but it was doubly exciting to learn that the tall, dark-haired girl—the one with the better figure, the one who looked so demure but who would beg, almost plead, to have him inside her again and again—was the daughter of an army brigadier in the Limassol staff headquarters.

For several days Nicos had gone on meeting them, and in the quieter moments the girls would tell him about themselves and their families. But it was to the dark-haired girl that he really listened. Soon he knew as much about the brigadier, his daily habits and routine, as did the man's own family. Using the information, Nicos

97

set an ambush for the brigadier as he drove home one evening to his bungalow on the outskirts of town. It was the one night of the week when he always returned driving his own car, unescorted. The brigadier died at the wheel, the car on its side in a ditch. There were three bullet holes in his chest, marked out in a circle where the heart had been. Nicos never saw the girls again, but he thought about them often.

On the fringes of Volos he saw a girl standing beside a bus stop. He whistled at her, pushing his head out the window, leering, laughing. The girl saw the expression on his face and turned her head away. Nicos tooted the horn and waved a hand. It was a good morning; there was the promise of much money today, and at night—who knew—perhaps another pretty girl like the one he had just seen.

Nicos was confident about his power over young women. He never missed an opportunity to use it, and it always worked. Of course he only went after the youngest. They were more impressionable, easier to dominate, to reduce to submission within a very short time. An older woman might have laughed at him. Since childhood he had feared being laughed at by a woman. He knew how to react to a man's mocking laugh. The few who had tried it over the years had been beaten to a pulp.

One, a young British airman, drunk in a Limassol bar, had laughed at his broken English. Nicos managed to contain his rage, finished his drink, and walked out. He had a good memory for faces. Two days later he saw the airman, with a sheaf of papers, leaving a store. He followed the man and watched him enter and leave several other shops before driving away in a Land Rover. Nicos knew enough of British Service habits to know the airman was making routine local purchase orders. The following week, on the same day and at the same time, the man was back in Limassol making an identical round of calls. Nicos was there too, watching, waiting for the right moment.

The airman's Land Rover was parked in a narrow side street close to a warehouse just off the main square. There was no one around when he returned to the vehicle. Nicos was waiting in a downstairs room of an abandoned house. He shot the man twice in the back of

98

the head, an easy target from across the street. The airman died instantly, still clutching the handle of the half-open door. Nicos went quickly through the house and left by the back door, cutting across an overgrown garden and slipping through a gate in a high wall. A dozen paces and he was back once again in the crowded main street that led to the square. As he passed the end of the side street, he glanced casually in the direction of the warehouse. A woman was screaming, pointing at the body slumped on its knees, head resting against the side of the Land Rover. Nicos had merely smiled to himself and walked on.

No woman had ever laughed at him—yet.

⩾ ⩾ ⩾

Nicos had a permanent stand for his taxi on a street close to the seafront almost midway between the Bank of Greece building and the yacht harbor. It was a good spot, shared only by two other taxis. People knew they could hire the Makrinitsá taxi here, and there were numerous opportunities for other fares. Visitors to Volos usually walked along the traffic-free promenade to watch the shipping in the harbor and to see the arrival and departure of cargo vessels and steamers serving the islands of Skiathos, Alonissos, and Skopelos. Passengers from these vessels often arrived in Volos to visit relatives and were anxious not to waste time waiting for buses to take them to the country districts.

There were no other taxis in the stand and few people about when Nicos arrived. He got out of the Mercedes and walked across the promenade toward the sea wall. Lighting a cigarette, he sat on the stonework and gazed out across the harbor, looking through the tangle of masts and pennants above the decks of brightly painted yachts toward the berths used by the steamers. There was a vessel in the anchorage used by the Sporades Islands line; on her bows in white letters was the name *Kyknos,* the Swan. Nicos knew the names of all the island steamers, when they sailed, when they arrived, which islands they stopped at. The *Kyknos* had come in from Skiathos, the island closest to the mainland southeast of the gulf. She made daily crossings.

The steamer had only just arrived, and a line of people were filing

99

down the gangway onto the quay. He could see figures embracing and heard faintly a murmur of voices and occasional bursts of laughter. Farther away, dwarfed by two massive cranes straddling the quay alongside her, was the *Fontana Amorosa*. Nicos watched the jibs of the cranes hoist bundles of planks away from the holds and the ship's deck and lift them, swinging and turning, into the air, then lower them effortlessly toward the gangs of dockers who waited to unleash the chains and hooks, making them ready to swing aloft again for the next load.

Amid the cries of the sea birds circling and swooping above the harbor came the sounds of chains rattling, metal banging on metal, men shouting and laughing, the constant revving and throbbing of the cranes' engines, and, humming like some demented bee, the high-pitched buzz of an outboard motor on a dinghy racing out of the harbor. The spreading wake left by the boat foamed out across the calm water. Moments later came several metallic clicks as masts touched, shivered, then touched again and the yachts at their moorings dipped and bobbed on the swell.

Nicos turned away to gaze for a time up and down the promenade. To his left, dominating the surrounding buildings and with a commanding view of the inner harbor, was the town hall, while in the distance to his right, equally imposing against the skyline, the Church of St. Constantine stood resolutely facing the sea. Behind this he could see the sunlight reflected on the roof of the Archaeological Museum. Alongside the building the leaves of chestnut and plane trees shimmered green and yellow, rippling gently in the face of a light wind blowing in from the gulf.

As Nicos glanced casually here and there along the seafront he saw signs that Volos was coming to life. Shops, offices, and cafés were opening their doors and the promenade was thronged with hurrying figures. From the street curving around one end of the promenade arose more traffic noise as the number of cars and buses increased; horns blared, gears clashed noisily, bicycle bells jangled. Nicos paid particular attention to the sound of the bicycle bells. There was always the chance of catching a glimpse of a pretty girl going past. He saw one now, weaving among a line of cars held up behind a slow-moving truck. He sucked in an appreciative breath; it was a student, her satchel of books bouncing against the lower part of her back. His eyes were fixed on her as she cycled across the path of the vehicles going in the opposite direction and vanished rapidly up a street beside the offices of the Sea Transport Agency.

Nicos was imagining the long, slender legs under the black skirt that had hidden them from his view and savoring what he had seen—the surge of the girl's breasts against the crisp, white blouse, and the clear, unblemished face, bright eyes, and long jet black hair—when suddenly he became aware that someone was watching him.

He turned his head slowly. Almost directly opposite, on the far side of the promenade, a young woman was moving to take the arm of a man standing a few paces behind her. They stood quite still for several seconds in front of a shop window displaying pottery and leather goods. The woman was holding the man's right arm, just below the elbow. He was leaning his head toward her so that she could whisper in his ear. Nicos realized he was looking at Maria Pierides.

It was his first sight of her since that night in the farmhouse when he and his brothers had killed her English lover. He had brought together all his hatred of the British on that occasion; of all his killings, that one had been the most satisfying. The young pig of an English officer had deserved to die. If Nicos had been allowed to do as he pleased, Maria would have finished up the same way for daring to play fast and loose with tradition, for having mocked Stephanides and the family name by whoring with someone whom any self-respecting Greek Cypriot, man or woman, should have recognized as an enemy of the people.

When Jonathan Barker had died, the terrified, incredulous expression on Maria's face, her attempts to shut out the sound of the revolver shots by covering her ears, her wails of despair had given Nicos the greatest feeling of power he had ever felt in his entire life. Now, as he recognized the small, slender figure and tried to calculate why she should turn up here—in Volos, of all places—he felt an inexplicable ache deep in the pit of his stomach, an ache he

101

would not admit as being fear. Just the same, it was there, that first, faint trace of apprehension.

This unease changed quickly to real fear, almost terror, when Nicos saw Maria's companion straighten up and look across the promenade. For what seemed like a minute Nicos felt the man's eyes on him, scrutinizing, staring. And though some distance separated them, Nicos was well aware of the depth of the other's contempt. At first he tried hard to recall the man's face, but as the eyes burned into him he was forced to avert his stare. He prided himself on his memory for faces. Where had he seen it before? Then, like the sudden clamp of a cold hand on his skin, the truth shot through his mind. He glanced back. The man's face was now in profile. Nicos saw the finely shaped nose—and he remembered Jonathan Barker; a much younger face, different eyes, fairer hair, but the same distinctive nose.

He saw Maria and the man turn once more to stare quite boldly in his direction. It was as if they were daring him, defying him to make some move. He slid off the wall, preparing for confrontation. But they turned and walked on, arm in arm, then without looking at him again went into a café. Nicos remained staring at the red-and-white awning over the frontage, gaping, unwilling to believe the reality of the situation, still certain he had been dreaming it all. But the fear was strong in him now, a fear that intensified the more he tried to reason why she should have come to Greece, and with this man in particular. No woman had ever laughed at him. No woman had ever dared, until a minute ago. But Maria Pierides had been laughing, a knowing, contemptuous laugh. It had been the sort of laugh Nicos had often used himself when he had silently terrified and humiliated a potential victim. The skin around his eyes and mouth had crinkled to allow that victim to take the measure of his victor's superior power.

Lost in thought, Nicos did not hear the voice close to his shoulder. He jumped as a hand reached out to touch his arm and a shadow fell across the promenade. Spinning around, he saw an old man looking at him. A battered brown suitcase was clutched in the old man's left hand, and the skin across his knuckles was stretched

102

white, almost transparent. Nicos stared at the hand. The fingers reminded him of claws. In the distance, close to his Mercedes, two other men and a woman, all carrying shopping bags, stood in silence, watching.

"Are you the taxi driver for Makrinitsá?" asked the old man.

Nicos nodded several times as if to clear his head.

"We want to go there. There is a wedding. We are relations of the bride."

Nicos told the old man to follow him, then started to walk slowly toward the car. Behind him the man's heavy shoes scraped on the flagstones. Nicos looked over once again in the direction of the café. There was no sign of Maria and the man, and because of the shade from the awning it was impossible to see through the long, high window fronting the promenade. But he imagined they were there, seated at a table right in front, watching, talking about him.

The sun was now climbing steadily in a sky of pure cobalt. A harsh white light was reflected from land and sea. Already it was hot, and in his armpits came the first trickles of sweat. But despite the heat his skin felt clammy and the sweat, now running in cold, uncomfortable rivulets down each side of his chest, was the sweat of fear.

≥ ≥ ≥

Within an hour of seeing Nicos on the Volos seafront, Richard and Maria were on their way to Makrinitsá by bus. The Greek Cypriot's Mercedes was in the parking lot when they arrived. Many of the passengers were elderly, and friends and relatives were gathered in force to meet them. Richard and Maria waited until the last of their companions had alighted before leaving the bus themselves.

The parking lot had been cut out from the side of a hill and was surrounded by trees. All vehicles had to be left there, as the houses in the village rose in tiers on the mountainside and there were no roads, merely paths. One track led to the square about two hundred yards away, on which a vehicle could run with difficulty, but a large notice announced that driving was prohibited there except in emergency. A long line of people stretched toward the village.

103

There were laughter and the carefree shouting of children, the sounds of happy people preparing to celebrate. A number of paths ran up the side of the mountain from the parking lot. On one, winding toward a group of houses a short distance away from the main part of the village, two men were leading several donkeys laden with bulging sacks.

Richard and Maria walked over to the Mercedes parked alongside a blue Ford, which also displayed a meter. They stood for several seconds staring at the dust-covered car.

"This is the one," said Maria, pointing to the Mercedes.

"And the other taxi?" asked Richard.

Maria shook her head.

"I don't know. I expect it also belongs to his cousin. But this is the one I saw parked not far from where Nicos was standing on the seafront this morning. He drove away in it after we went into the café. Didn't you notice?"

"No, I'm afraid I didn't. I was still recovering from the shock of having come across him so quickly after our arrival. Somehow I hadn't expected it would be so easy to find him, even though you knew of his whereabouts."

"Well, Richard, I took particular notice." Maria reached out to touch the car. Her fingers left a pattern on the film of dust. "This is the car. It is up to you now."

Richard nodded, looking thoughtful. Events were moving much faster than he had anticipated. It was hard to concentrate. The outline of their plan was already fixed in his mind, but to put it into practice required clear, logical thought. By now the passengers from the bus had almost reached the village. The sound of their voices and laughter drifted toward him. There was no one else in the lot except the bus driver, who was still seated behind the steering wheel of his vehicle. A light breeze floated down from the top of the mountain, rippling the leaves of the quince trees and hazel bushes and bringing with it the tinkling of the small bells of grazing sheep. Richard was aware of the silence and beauty surrounding him. At the same time, there was no escaping the ominous quality about the peace and beauty, which had undertones of death.

"You realize how dangerous this is going to be," he said to Maria, who was now staring in the direction of the village square. She turned her head, smiling a little, pleased by his concern.

"Oh, yes. I know. But I was scared stiff when we faced Andreas in the copper mine. I managed then; I can do it again."

"But this time you'll be on your own for a time. For how long depends on you—and on Nicos. I won't be able to help you if anything goes wrong."

She touched his arm.

"Don't worry, Richard. You worry too much. We are in this together. We share the risks. It was my own idea to act as a . . . how did you call it?"

"A decoy."

"Yes, a decoy. I'll see to it that nothing goes wrong."

"I'm still of the opinion it might be better to do the job right here, then get the hell out as quickly as possible. There would be fewer complications and it would be less likely that something unexpected might happen."

"You know, Richard, for someone who is supposed to be a hard-headed, successful businessman, you sometimes seem unable to make up your mind. This is a small village—I have already told you that. Since everybody knows everyone else here and is aware of what they're doing, I think the risks would be too great—more so, perhaps, now that we know so many people will be taking part in the wedding festivities. You heard them all talking about it on the bus. At least I can mingle with local people and the visitors to the village. As an Englishman you would be noticed."

Richard laughed. "Point taken. I'll say no more about it. Let's just get on with what we decided we'd do."

An engine roared behind them and they turned to see the bus moving slowly out of the parking lot. The driver smiled and waved. Maria lifted a hand in response.

"Good," Richard said. "I was hoping he'd go away before long. It makes my task much easier. Only remember—you must find him quickly. Stop him even if other people want to hire him."

She nodded. "I understand."

105

"Then what are we waiting for?"

"You tell me."

"We're ready. Take care."

"And you, Richard. I hope I will not be too long."

"So do I."

They parted, he walking slowly around the lot, watching in case anyone should be on the hillside, she strolling casually along the stony track toward the square and the scattered houses of Makrinitsá, their white walls and red-tiled roofs glaring in the fierce light of the sun.

≥ ≥ ≥

Nicos was in the square when he saw Maria emerge from a lane and halt close to the low railings around a well. He was sitting on a red bench beneath an enormous plane tree, the girth of its trunk so immense that the interior was taken up by a cobbler's shop, its doorway cut into the side. Above his head the branches and foliage interlocked with the spreading limbs of other trees to provide a canopy of shade across the entire square. Here and there, narrow shafts of sunlight filtered through the branches to touch the worn flagstones with splashes of diffused color. On the fringes of the square, seated around tables in front of the cafés and *tavernas*, were groups of people drinking coffee and wine, talking loudly, laughing.

Nicos was not surprised to see Maria. He had expected she would turn up sooner or later here in Makrinitsá. He had no clear reason for knowing why this should be so; it was intuition born of fear. Despite his past acts of bravado and missions of ruthlessness, on this occasion Nicos Tengerakis was afraid.

It was not the fear that grips a man when he faces a gun or is forced to proceed into battle through a hail of bullets; it was much deeper, more paralyzing. Its effect was all the greater because Nicos had never before experienced real fear. In his various encounters with death in Cyprus he had always held a position of mastery, of complete domination over his victims. Nicos understood weapons and physical strength and could deal with them. But his intellect could comprehend only the obvious. Once challenged by superior

106

thinking, by someone whose opposition was not embodied in open violence, his façade cracked. Ever since Nicos had seen Maria and her companion in Volos, his self-confidence had slowly been eroding. It was now almost completely gone; he felt trapped, deeply worried, no longer in control. There was no way he knew of halting the process. This fear was intangible, and he could only deal with tangible things.

When he saw Maria enter the square he remembered the contemptuous expression on her face earlier that day. Since then, as his fear mounted, he had been haunted by the memory of how she had stared at him and of the man who was an older version of the dead English officer. On Nicos's return to Makrinitsá he had parked his taxi and gone to sit in the square, first outside a café where he had drunk some coffee, then in the shade beneath the plane tree. He had tried to resolve the situation, to come to terms with the shock he had received. But the longer he allowed his mind to linger over the past and the uncertainty raised by Maria's presence here in Greece, the more confused he became. He made no efforts to seek fares for his taxi. He sat alone in a daze, head aching, brain numbed. And as he sat, his body longed for some release from the fear within him, a cloying, indefinable fear that threatened to smother him.

The square was rapidly filling with people preparing for a day of open-air celebrations to honor the couple from the village who would be married on Sunday. Already a group of musicians had started to play, the tremulous sounds of bouzouki and guitar shimmering among the trees, accompanied by a rising volume of hand clapping in time to the music. For a moment Nicos lost sight of Maria as several women carrying baskets of food and wine surrounded her, then passed in procession toward the far side of the square.

Maria had not expected to find Nicos quite so easily. She had imagined herself searching the narrow lanes of Makrinitsá, being forced to ask people for directions to the house of Nicos Tengerakis, steadily making herself more conspicuous by pretending to be part of the village while displaying obvious signs that she was not. Now she was no more than just another face in the crowd. There were so many new faces in Makrinitsá today that no one would ever remember her.

She saw Nicos's seated figure and was aware of his eyes fastened almost hypnotically on her from across the square. She felt her heart pounding, and her ears shut out the sound of the music, voices, and laughter all around her, while she concentrated on what she had to do.

Several couples were dancing directly in front of Maria, and she dodged them. An old man supported by two walking sticks stumbled against her as she passed. She smiled and put out a hand to steady him. He turned his bearded face and gazed at her for several seconds with sad gray eyes. They nodded to each other, then he shuffled slowly away while she turned back in time to see Nicos rising to his feet. Afraid he might be preparing to leave, she called his name.

"Nicos!"

She was surprised by the stridency and strength of her voice as it rose above the noise in the square. Nicos looked around and their eyes met. She was close enough now to see the tension in his face, the gaunt, haunted expression that was the first expression of fear. In that moment she felt a surge of confidence, the pent-up hate and loathing exploding inside her, driving her forward to ignite the chain of events that would lead to his death.

"Hello, Nicos," she said. He murmured something in reply, but his voice was so low she failed to understand the words. "I have to speak with you."

He stared impassively. She might have been a stranger.

"What have we to speak about?" He gave a brief, hollow laugh. "Don't tell me you have come all the way to Greece just to talk with me."

"No," Maria replied, smiling now, fully aware of her power. She could see he was deeply worried, could sense the aura of fear that surrounded him. It exuded from his body like a smell, as obvious as the sweat from the pores of his skin. She grew bolder, knowing instinctively she was responsible for this fear. She had always suspected that of the three Tengerakis brothers Nicos was the coward; now she was certain of it. She shook her head.

"No, Nicos. I am on holiday. Aboard a ship. As we were in Volos, I thought I would find you. I wanted——"

"We?"

"What do you mean?"

"You said 'we.' Who was that man I saw you with this morning on the seafront in Volos? Are you traveling with him?"

"Oh, him. No—he is only another passenger on the ship. We went out walking together. He is——"

"Why did you not speak to me this morning? Why come here looking for me?"

"There was no time to speak then," Maria said. "I have plenty of time now. Plenty of time to talk about Stephanides, and the future. I have heard nothing from him since he went to England. I wanted to get in touch with him. You must know where he is living."

"Why come here to ask me this? They could have told you in Trimithousa."

Maria looked down at her feet and spoke in a low voice.

"After what happened I felt I could not go back there. I did not want to meet Andreas. I am afraid of him."

"Yet you are not afraid of me?"

She looked up then, staring hard at his face. When she spoke he was forced to avert his eyes.

"No. I was afraid—once. But not now. I have nothing to fear from you. I had a holiday from school and I wanted to see Greece, so I came here on a ship."

"But you have been here before. You came here with the English boy——"

"When did you hear about that?"

Nicos's casual remark had shaken her. She was momentarily confused and, for the first time since her arrival in Makrinitsá, unsure of herself.

"How did you know?"

Nicos shrugged his shoulders. He did not reply. His lips were a thin line, his gaze directed fully on her now, the narrowed eyes conveying contempt for her obvious discomfort.

Maria made a helpless gesture with her arms.

"What does it matter? That was in the past," she said, the words bitter on her tongue, hating him for forcing her to remember, hating herself for what she went on to say. "It is forgotten. He is best forgotten."

Nicos smiled ingratiatingly.

"Ah. You have seen your error. You now regret your affair—your attachment to an enemy of our people."

"Yes," she said, the sound of her words of betrayal cutting deep within her, her inner torment no less despite the necessary lie.

"You admit you were foolish?"

"I was foolish."

The words were loathsome both to say and to hear.

"Good," he said. "You should have admitted that a long time ago. You could have been spared much trouble. We could all have been spared much trouble."

The square was now thronged with people laughing and dancing, eating, drinking, and talking. Wave upon wave of voices swelled up between the houses and *tavernas* and mingled with the pulsating rhythm of the music. A singer had joined the musicians, long black hair billowing over her shoulders as she swayed in the center of the square, surrounded by dancers and small children laughing and shrieking and clapping their hands. The bride and groom, both in their twenties, arrived accompanied by their families. They stood on opposite sides of the square smiling at each other across the heads of their excited relatives. Glasses of wine and ouzo were constantly raised in their direction. They acknowledged the toasts with nods of the head, the girl's face slightly flushed, embarrassed by the extent and enthusiasm of the public acclamation.

"It is so noisy here," said Maria, glancing around the crowd, then back toward Nicos.

He stared at her for several seconds, then replied, "We could go to my house. It is there, up on the hill at the back of the village."

Maria looked at him steadily. What she now had to say had to be expressed with the maximum conviction, the correct degree of emphasis presented in a casual fashion so as not to arouse suspicion.

"Perhaps we might go back to Volos? We could talk in your car. It would be more private."

110

She managed to smile at him, at the same time hating herself for her display of friendship and the lies she had told denouncing Jonathan's memory. But all these were necessary evils, to ensure revenge for the evil once unleashed against her.

Nicos frowned for a moment, then, as he looked once again at the small, attractive figure of the girl alongside him, he saw the extent of her beauty. He could appreciate why his younger brother Stephanides was determined to fulfill the bargain between the families that she should be his wife. He felt the tension oozing out of him. What, after all, had he to fear from her?

"Yes," he said. "I will drive you to Volos." He waved an arm at the scene around them in the square. "The celebrations have only just begun. There must be many more people who want to come to Makrinitsá today. I should be in Volos keeping my taxi busy. Come."

They walked side by side through the crowd, away from the shade and the music and the sound of voices, out into the oppressive glare of the sun. There were several people on the track walking slowly toward the village. A couple of men nodded casually to Nicos, who lifted a hand to acknowledge their greeting. Maria walked purposefully, aware of her mounting fear that something might go wrong. The next few minutes were crucial.

She had no wish to look at Nicos, nor at the sunlit beauty of the surrounding countryside: at the distant blue of the sea, the tops of trees in the valleys, vague shapes of buildings in Volos, and houses on the plain around the gulf appearing gray amid the shimmering heat haze; the donkeys and sheep on the hillside above her; the droning of bees and insects among the flowers on the banks alongside the track; the scent of herbs rich and fragrant on the soft mountain breeze. She ignored all these things, her eyes and mind focused on the parking lot, the black Mercedes, and whether or not Richard had carried out his part of their plan.

There was no sign of him. That was as it should be. But had he finished? Had he even been able to start work and, if so, to continue undisturbed? Had she given him enough time? Maria had no way of knowing the answers, and this increased her tension. She had set a

111

trap to catch Nicos Tengerakis, but unless every detail dovetailed exactly, she herself would be caught—trapped without any hope of help, alone with the man she wanted to kill.

"One moment."

In a daze Maria heard the Greek Cypriot's voice, then a hand on her arm forced her to halt. Oh, God, had he spotted something? What had he seen? She turned to Nicos, who was staring at the parking lot, a thoughtful expression on his face. He fumbled in a trouser pocket and produced several keys.

"Good," he said. "We will take the other taxi, the Ford. I have the key with me."

Maria stared at him, feeling a wave of helplessness engulf her. It was all going wrong; she knew that from this moment on it would all go horribly wrong.

"But why?"

"Something was wrong with the Mercedes when I came back from Volos this morning. It's nothing—but my cousin's taxi is here. He is on holiday. We will use his car for this journey." He laughed. "It is not as grand a car as the Mercedes, but . . ."

He shrugged his shoulders and laughed again. The sound sent a cold spasm along Maria's spine. She had no choice but to walk with Nicos toward the blue Ford, knowing Richard was not far away, watching them, waiting for the right moment to act, for the moment that would now never materialize. And all the time there was nothing she could do to warn him, no single thing she could think of to help herself. To act foolishly now would reveal her intentions and betray them both.

≥ ≥ ≥

Richard watched from the middle of a thicket of bushes close to the Mercedes. He was certain nothing could go wrong. It had been a relatively simple matter to open the driver's door of the taxi with a short piece of wire, a skill he had acquired from a traveling sales representative who persisted in losing his car key. Then, leaning inside, he had unlocked the rear doors so that once the Mercedes was

112

on the move it would be possible for him to rush at the car and jump inside. Surprise was the key to the operation's success, that and luck, the ability to get into the vehicle without being seen by anyone. He judged the first part to be easy; afterward, with a knife at the Greek Cypriot's neck, he would be in complete control. He prayed no one would come into the parking lot at the vital moment. But even if anyone did turn up he would still have to go ahead. By then he would have committed himself. He had not been able to relock the driver's door, but this point didn't worry him. He doubted if Nicos would spend much time puzzling over it when he returned to the Mercedes. The Greek Cypriot would have too much on his mind after Maria's sudden appearance.

Richard kept quite still as he saw them approach along the track from the village. He wondered what Maria had already said to Nicos, how he had reacted to seeing and talking to her once again, with the memory of that hateful night in Cyprus uppermost in their minds. Although he was tense inside, it was not with the tension of fear, but the tautness of nerves and muscles eager for action.

Richard saw Nicos stop and stare in the direction of the parking lot, then halt Maria by placing a hand on her arm. For a moment it was as if the two faces were looking directly at him, and despite the cover provided by the bushes he felt exposed. They were talking, and the Greek Cypriot was gesticulating with an arm; then they were coming toward him, and when Maria was close enough he was able to see an expression of disbelief, almost panic, on her face. She was looking around with an air of desperation as Nicos and she came level with the two taxis.

When Richard saw the Greek Cypriot open the driver's door of the blue Ford, he grasped the reason for Maria's agitation. He watched with mounting alarm as Nicos opened the front passenger door and motioned to Maria to get into the car. The thump of the doors had a ring of finality, leaving a peculiar sense of stillness in the air. It was as if time itself were standing still while Richard's judgment and reaction hung suspended on a delicate balance. The engine started up and the Ford reversed a little, then swung around,

113

going past him parallel to the clump of bushes. He had a fleeting glimpse of Maria's face—head turning, eyes staring—and the Greek Cypriot's profile; within seconds all that was left was the memory of this sight and a cloud of dust obliterating the car as it turned onto the mountain road.

Richard ran up the slope and tugged open the driver's door of the Mercedes. He was surprised how easy it was, despite his confusion and fumbling fingers, to insert the piece of wire into the ignition switch and turn it on. The engine burst into life at the second attempt. He manipulated the gear lever, failing for several seconds to find reverse. A number of times the taxi moved forward, threatening to plunge over the lip of the bank and onto the wooded slope; then, engine roaring, the Mercedes shot backward almost to the center of the lot before it came to a halt. The engine stalled and refused to start again, and at once Richard had a vision of the futility of what he was attempting to do, the consequences of failure not only for himself but for Maria, now somewhere on the winding road beneath him.

He cursed and tried again. There was a sputter of life from the engine, then silence. This happened three more times, while sweat poured from his face and armpits, before there was enough power for him to release the clutch and press firmly down on the accelerator. The taxi responded willingly now, bounding forward. The engine ran smoothly as he changed up into second gear and turned sharply onto the road.

There were distant shouts. Richard glanced in the rear-view mirror and saw two figures on the track between the parking lot and Makrinitsá. They were waving their arms; one was standing still while the other came on in pursuit before halting in the middle of the open space. Their shouts were inaudible. He had no way of knowing if they were merely annoyed at having seen the taxi drive away without them or if they had seen him steal the car. He didn't care. Nothing mattered now except catching up to the blue Ford. And then?

There were no thoughts of failure in his mind, only a frantic attempt to assess the new dangers and surmount the difficulties in what now seemed a hopeless task.

≥ ≥ ≥

"Treacherous bitch."

The words exploded from the Greek Cypriot's mouth with such venom that for a moment Maria was gripped by an uncontrollable spasm of terror. Her eyes left the landscape sliding past the fast-moving car and focused on Nicos's face. He did not look at her, his eyes wavering between the road and the rear-view mirror. She twisted around in her seat to see the Mercedes closing rapidly on them. When she turned away, not daring to look at Nicos, her eyes fastening on the winding ribbon of road, she heard him repeat, "Treacherous bitch. I believed you. I really did believe you."

Behind the anger in his voice Maria detected a strain of fear. Somehow this diminished her own fear. She heard herself say, "I'm glad. You were meant to believe me. I only wish everything else had gone according to plan. By now you might have been dead."

Nicos braked fiercely, then swung the car into a tight left-hand bend. The tires squealed on the road surface, slipping a little, fighting for grip. Maria recoiled as the Ford mounted the verge and veered in toward the low stone wall. She could see the tops of the trees far below, the red-tiled roofs of several houses. Nicos expertly corrected the skid. The wall vanished and all four wheels were back on the road again. The car raced forward. The road was straight for at least three-quarters of a mile.

Nicos was laughing now. The sound of his laughter and the shock of having survived what had seemed an inevitable crash—a sudden plunge by the Ford through the stone wall down into the valley—made Maria want to scream. The urge to do so rose in her throat like mounting nausea. She fought hard to suppress it, choking back the sounds so that when they escaped they were like muffled sobs.

"Bitch. You'll regret this," Nicos growled.

Maria turned her head and stared hard at the hated figure beside her. The sound of his laughter had faded away. The corners of his

115

mouth were twitching, and on his features an expression of wild determination shone with the intensity of an uncontrollable fear. She saw the film of sweat on his face, the white knuckles gripping the rim of the steering wheel, the hunched frame leaning forward. His body seemed wracked by fear and anger, mingling emotions that threatened to engulf him. Despite her terror of the speed at which they were traveling, of what might happen to her, the sight of the Greek Cypriot's fear, his coward's agony, eased her own burden. There was renewed strength in her voice when she said, "You evil bastard. You deserve everything that's coming to you. Even if I have to die myself, I'll be happy knowing you have perished as well."

They passed two cars parked among trees close to the road. There was a blur of faces, then Nicos's face was turned toward her and Maria saw the lips drawn back. A snarl came from his half-open mouth and he punched at her with his right hand. She ducked her head and the blow missed. The Ford lurched violently, wheels chewing the soft earth of the bank. He punched again, and this time his clenched fist struck her a glancing blow on the side of the neck. Instinctively she thrust both arms in his direction, rising up from the seat to slap at his face, his neck, his chest. As he tried to protect himself, both hands left the steering wheel.

The car wobbled, then snaked onto the bank. The impact forced it sideways back onto the road with front wheels slewing, carrying it forward toward the opposite side. They both realized in the same moment what was likely to happen. Maria let go of his shirt and the Greek Cypriot's hands went back to the steering wheel, fingers tightening around the rim, wrenching and tugging, right foot pumping the brake pedal. He pulled the nose of the Ford away from the wall, but the rear end scraped against the stonework, smashing and tearing, sending mortar and rocks into the valley.

They were now on a tight hairpin bend, a left-hand turn, then a sharp right. Maria watched horrified as the speedometer needle banged erratically beneath its glass fascia and the car shuddered, tires protesting, as Nicos stabbed at the brake pedal and spun the steering wheel to force the taxi into the sharp curves of the roadway. The Ford went into the right-hand bend on the wrong side of the

116

road. At once a great shape loomed in front of the windshield. They both cried out simultaneously, and as Maria's hands went up to cover her face, Nicos twisted the steering wheel so violently that the taxi lurched, seeming to leap into the air. For a moment the Ford appeared to be in danger of toppling onto its side.

They missed the front of the bus by several inches. A horn blew, long and sustained, and faces peered down at them as they went past, almost brushing the coachwork of the massive vehicle. The road was straight once again and Nicos was accelerating. When Maria looked back the bus was stationary, as if frozen to the bend. She saw the Mercedes driving past it. She could still hear the horn blaring and with it the sound of another horn, sounding in staccato bursts. Nicos, too, appeared to hear it. Although she could not have believed it possible, Maria felt the Ford's speed increasing. Now the wind was screaming at the edges of the windows and inside her head was the constant sound of wind and horns and the harsh, almost hysterical gasps of the Greek Cypriot's breathing.

Nicos swore loudly as he saw in the rear-view mirror the shape of the Mercedes gaining ground. He pressed the accelerator to its limit; the Ford would go no faster. In the side mirrors he watched transfixed as Richard started to flash the headlights on the Mercedes. There was something hypnotic about the sudden blazing of yellow beams in the harsh sunlight, off and on, off and on, the glare alternating with the rapid blaring of the horn. Time and again Nicos found his eyes drawn away from the road to gaze in fascinated horror at the reflection in the mirrors as the black hulk of the Mercedes drew closer every second, edging out into the center of the road, preparing to overtake him.

Nicos cursed the Ford for its sluggishness, cursed Maria, swore at the Englishman so eager to take revenge, but above all, cursed himself for his own ineptitude, his inability to escape from certain death.

Richard was now holding one hand down on the button of the horn, handling the Mercedes with confidence as he crept within feet of the rear of the Ford. He swung left, intending to pass. The sound of the horn was boring into the Greek Cypriot's brain, shredding his

117

nerves, but he reacted quickly to the shadow of the Mercedes looming up behind. A sudden turn of the steering wheel sent the Ford across the path of the pursuing car. The two taxis collided, the nose of the Mercedes smashing into the rear door of the Ford. There was a screech of tearing metal, then Richard accelerated the Mercedes, pushing the Ford aside, burrowing through between it and the high bank, the wheels throwing up dust and stones, earth and the tangled stems of flowers. The debris sprayed across the road.

Maria could see Richard quite clearly as she looked past Nicos at the black Mercedes now almost level with the Ford. She wanted desperately to do something to help, but despite her fear knew she was powerless to act. She wanted to close her eyes, but they refused to shut, drawn in terror to the low wall, only a few feet away from her side of the car, and the valleys and trees, boulders and emptiness below.

Nicos swerved, momentarily widening the gap between the Ford and the Mercedes. He was shouting at Richard, almost screaming, rage and hysteria bubbling from him now. When the Mercedes was slightly in front, starting to cut across his path, he turned the steering wheel and sent the Ford ramming against the black taxi. The two vehicles collided with a sickening lurch that sent Maria up out of her seat. The top of her head crashed against the roof.

The Mercedes was forced sideways, the impact knocking Richard's hands from the steering wheel. Nicos continued to ram the side of the Mercedes, battering the Ford against it, wrenching and twisting the steering wheel, swinging in and out, weaving from side to side, metal crunching and tearing, the noise of steel on steel resounding above the high-pitched roar of both engines. The Greek Cypriot was gradually succeeding in forcing the front of the Mercedes away from the road. Despite the other car's greater power, the Ford was now gaining ground.

The two taxis were traveling alongside each other, approaching a gently curving right-hand bend. Richard managed to regain his hold on the bucking steering wheel, but it was almost beyond him to control the car's direction. He tried to retaliate by turning the Mercedes in against the Ford, but a direct blow on the front passenger door sent the Mercedes swerving off the road. The momentum carried the taxi onto a bank running up at a steep angle. He was certain the vehicle would overturn, and he could see the Ford pulling away, going into the bend. He had almost regained control when one of the front wheels hit a rock. The Mercedes veered back onto the road and hurtled forward to smash into the rear of the Ford, the impact crushing the trunk and the wide bumper.

Inside the Ford, Maria felt the thump as the Mercedes hit them. She pitched forward, banging her forehead on the windshield. She put up her hands, pressing them against the roof. The Ford was spinning completely out of control. Sky, trees, roadway, walls, steep bank, all were a flying circle of blurred light. Nicos was twisting the steering wheel left and right, yelling at the top of his voice, as at last the true depths of his fear became completely audible, sickening her in her own moments of terror.

When the Ford seemed to settle it was pointing straight at the wall following the curve of the bend. Maria realized what was about to happen even before she heard the Greek Cypriot's final, dreadful scream and the hollow banging of his feet on the floor as he pumped at the brake pedal. For a moment the Ford seemed to reduce speed, then it shot forward and crashed into the wall.

Maria's fingers scratched at the cloth covering the roof, gained a grip, and held firm at the moment of impact. Rocks were sent flying on either side of the car. There was a loud banging noise from beneath the floor and the sound of glass smashing and splintering. For a moment the whole valley and the tops of the trees were spread out before her. The Ford stopped suddenly, the front dipping down, hanging over the edge of the slope, the rear wheels held by massive boulders still firmly embedded at the base of the wall.

There were seconds of noise and confusion, followed by silence but for the sound of gas slopping in the tank and the hiss as it dripped from the ruptured tank and touched the hot exhaust pipe, then ran in eager rivers along the floor of the car toward the engine. Though dazed by the blow and the shock, Maria saw Nicos halfway through the shattered windshield, slumped across the blue, dented hood of the Ford. His head was twisted awkwardly at an acute angle

119

to the rest of his body. His eyes were wide open and staring. There was blood on his face and hands. On one hand the fingers continued to twitch, drumming on the metalwork.

She heard Richard's voice and the sound of a door opening. He was helping her out onto the parapet, then down onto the road. Her legs felt dead, threatening to crumple under her weight. As she slumped against him he put his arms around her, supporting her against his own trembling body.

"Come on, Maria. Only a few more seconds. The road's empty. We must get away while there's still time. Now."

He dragged her, feet trailing, toward the battered Mercedes and pushed her inside. She felt faint and sick, but her senses revived a little when she heard a loud noise like a sudden intake of breath and at once saw tongues of flame burst from the engine of the Ford. Richard flung himself into the Mercedes and put the taxi into gear. As they went past the burning vehicle, black smoke was topping the scarlet of the leaping flames. Already the body of Nicos Tengerakis was alight, trousers and shirt burning fiercely. They gazed at it, feeling no pity; the vision of body and vehicle burning in front of their eyes goaded them into further haste, making them eager to be gone while the secret of what had happened was still theirs alone.

They said nothing as they descended the final sections of the mountain road. But at one point where it was possible to see through a gap in the trees, Richard slowed down and they both looked back. The Ford could not be seen, only a dense, dark cloud of smoke rising toward the blue sky. A short distance farther on they met a car starting the climb toward Makrinitsá, and they knew there was little time left to cover all traces of their connection with the flaming car several miles back on the mountainside.

≥ ≥ ≥

They abandoned the Mercedes in a quiet side street on the outskirts of Volos well away from the Makrinitsá road. There were several women standing talking among themselves a short distance away, but when they looked up the street toward the taxi, the couple were walking off in the opposite direction. Although Richard and

Maria wanted to get back on board the *Fontana Amorosa* as quickly as possible, it was still too early in the afternoon to do this without having to answer awkward questions from Captain Stavros.

They walked around Volos for a couple of hours, their nerves settling; then they ate moussaka and drank wine in a restaurant near the seafront. There, apart from the voices of other customers and the distant sounds of traffic, all was quiet and peaceful; the events of the past few hours seemed so far away they might have belonged to another age, another world. A large bruise had appeared on Maria's forehead where she had banged her head in the Ford, and as the discoloration spread, so too did the throbbing pain in her temple. They decided to go back to the harbor and face the raised eyebrows of Captain Stavros, who was sure to want to know why they had returned so soon when his vessel was only in the port for one day.

The captain was on the bridge watching the loading of the cargo for the return to Cyprus. They dodged the swinging jibs of the cranes and the men and trucks on the quay and climbed the gangway onto the deck. Captain Stavros appeared almost before they set foot on the ship. Holding Maria's arm, Richard forestalled the captain's anticipated question.

"Maria is very tired—a bad headache."

Captain Stavros nodded his head sympathetically, then saw the purple bruise on her forehead. Richard saw the captain's eyebrows raised, one hand pointing.

"A fall. It has spoiled our day."

"I am so sorry," said Stavros. "She must rest in your cabin. When she is settled you must join me for a drink and tell me what you have been doing today. It is a beautiful place. A great pity we are only here for such a short time."

Richard nodded while Maria smiled weakly at the captain. They went below. A seaman washing the deck in the shade of the bridge stared after them for several seconds before returning to work. He had seen the bruise on the girl's face and noticed how she trembled.

In the cabin Maria said, "Oh, God, I wish the ship would sail now. I just want to get away."

Richard put his arms around her and kissed her on the cheek. "It

121

won't be long now. Anyway, we're safe enough here. We've nothing to worry about. It will take the police a long time to get to the bottom of Nicos's accident." He smiled. "That's what it will look like, you know—an accident on a bad stretch of road. At first it will just appear as a very bad, but normal, car smash."

"And then?"

He shrugged his shoulders.

"A great mystery, I suppose. Where did his passenger get to? Why was his Mercedes stolen? Was it even stolen? If so, who stole it? But why should we worry? We will both be far away before they even get around to thinking along these lines. And with you in Cyprus and me in Britain and no one in these parts knowing us from Adam and Eve, we'll have nothing to concern ourselves over. You can stop worrying. It was all a bit of a shambles, I know. But we did achieve what we set out to do. Having done it, that's all that matters."

"It was horrible, Richard. Not even in the mine when Andreas was fighting with you was I as frightened as I was today. But"—Maria lay back on the bunk and rested her head on the pillow—"it was worth it. Worth every second of danger, just to see him dead."

"Revenge," said Richard. "It's like a disease that gets into the blood, a curse. In our case we'll be free of it only when Stephanides is dead. That will be easy after all the difficulties we've been through so far. In London I'll be on home territory. I'll have all the advantages."

"I want to come with you to London. I said I would help you——"

Richard placed a hand over her mouth.

"No. You must stay in Cyprus. Carry on normally—well, as best you can in the present circumstances, because no one knows what's likely to happen in Cyprus now. But you must go back to work and lead your usual life. I'll return to Britain immediately we get back to Limassol. That's the most sensible way for us to help each other. In the long run it will be for the best. You'll see."

122

≫≫≫**6**

⩾ ⩾ ⩾

But was it the best thing to have done? Was it really no more than wishful thinking on my part that Maria could be left behind in Cyprus to pick up the threads of her previous life? In view of what has happened since then, I often ask myself these questions.

Of course, in the circumstances, there was really little else I could have done. She was, after all, a citizen of Cyprus and would only have been able to enter Britain on a visitor's permit. She would eventually have had to return to her homeland. The danger would still have been there, as persistent and as strong as ever. A little foresight might have shown me that the best course to adopt would have been to persuade her to leave Cyprus for good and urge her to come live and work permanently in Britain. But at the time I was ignorant of the extent of the danger that might threaten her, and for that matter unaware of any danger that might affect me.

Even if I had been aware of any repercussions, such was the upheaval in Cyprus, because of the coup and the imminent Turkish invasion of the island, and so complicated was the process of sponsoring Maria for a work permit (and we could not learn, perhaps for several weeks, whether one would be granted) that I doubt very much if either of us could have withstood the added strain. It's so

125

easy to be wise after the event. If at the onset I had been aware of the result of my vendetta against the Tengerakis brothers, I would never have undertaken the mission. If after we had killed Andreas and Nicos I had stopped for a moment to consider the likely consequence, the possibility of discovery by the brothers' family, I would have abandoned any attempt to kill the third brother. But the time is long past for regret; it is now too late. What happened was unavoidable once the chain of events was set in motion; some deep-seated, compulsive force willed it—and I obeyed. So when the *Fontana Amorosa* docked in Limassol harbor after the voyage from Greece, the thought uppermost in my mind was how quickly I could get back to Britain and get rid of the remaining brother, Stephanides.

Cyprus was in a state of complete turmoil. Since we had been away, events had moved swiftly to involve Greek and Turk alike. There had been bitter fighting, especially in the north, in and around Nicosia. No longer was the question debated whether the Turkish government in Ankara might order an invasion; now the question was when it would happen. Nicos Sampson, now president in place of the deposed Makarios, was becoming aware that what he had started in liaison with the Greek colonels in Athens, whose influence was strong among the officers of the Cypriot National Guard, had gone much further than anyone had foreseen. Attempts were being made to replace Sampson, Archbishop Makarios was touring the world's capitals seeking support for his own return to power, and out of it all had emerged the familiar pattern of the island's bloody history: Greek at war with Greek, championing individual philosophies and causes, the Turkish community trapped in the middle, fighting back, spurred on by the promise of invasion from the mainland.

British residents and visitors to the island were advised to go to the British Sovereign Base area south of Limassol at Akrotiri where, because of the closing of the civil airport at Nicosia, the Royal Air Force was using its fleet of transport aircraft to mount an evacuation.

I went back with Maria to her flat in Limassol and tried to telephone Christos Charalambous, but there was no reply at his office.

When I tried again to reach him it was impossible even to get a telephone link with Nicosia. Before going to Greece, I had removed my belongings from the seafront hotel in Limassol and left them in Maria's flat. When I had come south from Nicosia to trace Maria, I had signed out of the Hotel Imperial and taken my luggage with me, meaning to reregister on my return. In retrospect it had been one of my more prudent moves.

So there was nothing to prevent my turning up at Akrotiri and requesting a flight back to Britain. Well, only one thing: the car I had hired in Nicosia for my original weekend trip to Limassol. I decided that the company would have to whistle for it. After all, I wasn't trying to steal it, and in the circumstances it was logical to use it to drive to the Akrotiri RAF base. Anyway, almost every hour, the announcer on the British Forces Broadcasting wavelength kept exhorting British citizens to use every means at their disposal to make the journey to Akrotiri. I wasn't going to ignore useful advice.

Saying good-bye to Maria was much more difficult than I'd imagined it would be. A bond of affection and trust had been established between us during our time together. On the return voyage to Cyprus we had not repeated our earlier desperate bout of lovemaking. We had not even slept together; not because we didn't desire each other, but because that single night had been born of the moment, when the tension and strain had sent us into each other's arms. We were not ashamed of what we had done. We were adult enough to accept the baser aspects of human desire and relationships. But from start to finish our alliance needed no physical expression to endure. Ours was a bond of shared determination and faith in the other's capabilities, linked by the single will to destroy those who had removed from our lives a person whose love was common to us both.

Daylight was fading quickly and I was anxious to get on my way to Akrotiri, a drive from Limassol of about eight miles. But I lingered in the flat, using up precious minutes, drinking cup after cup of coffee that Maria insisted on making, as if in her own way she were trying to delay my departure.

"Take care, Richard," she said, as for the fifth or sixth time I

127

rose to my feet to stare aimlessly through the open window. "Stephanides is more cunning than the other two. He has a sharp brain. Being the youngest, he is more nimble, more athletic. He is very dangerous."

I gave a weak laugh, my mind on the more immediate problem of how I was going to account to my wife for more than a week of silence from Cyprus. True, after the coup had taken place, I had asked Christos's secretary to cable Felicity to say I was safe. But she would have read in the newspapers and seen on television what had been happening on the island, and there had been no further message from me. As far as I knew, the evacuation of British citizens had been going on for several days. By now she was probably worried stiff, and all the while I had been cruising in the Mediterranean and the Aegean and chasing around Greece to kill a man.

I crossed the room to where Maria was standing in the kitchen doorway, coffee pot in one hand. I took it from her and placed it on a table. Then I took her small body into my arms and held her tight. I kissed her briefly on the mouth and several times on the cheek, but there was no passion in it. Our embrace was that of a devoted brother and sister about to part, perhaps never to see each other again.

"I wish I were going with you," she said when we separated, her eyes heavy and her body trembling as she fought hard to hold back the tears.

"We've already been over that ground several times," I said, perhaps a trifle sharply. I saw her eyes widen and a frown cross her features. Reaching forward, I patted her arm. "Sorry, but it's just not possible. Certainly not in the middle of this present upheaval. I'll let you know when the job is done. Just as soon as——"

"Make him suffer, Richard. He deserves it—perhaps even more than the other two brutes. I saw the hatred in his eyes when he tortured Jonathan. I have a similar hate—reserved solely for him."

I stared for several seconds at her face, now transformed into a rigid mask. Her eyes were burning with a determined ferocity.

"You would really like to kill him yourself, wouldn't you?"

She nodded slowly. "More than anything," she said.

128

"I'll make a good job of it," I replied. "For both of us."

"You have the address in London?"

"Yes. Tucked safely away in my wallet. Don't worry about me. Save your worry for yourself here in Cyprus."

"I think invasion is very near now," she said. "The Turkish government has threatened it many times before. But this time I think they will act. Things have gone too far for them to remain idle."

"For God's sake, keep out of trouble, whatever happens. There's no knowing what will be the outcome if serious fighting starts."

"I expect I'll survive. I'm young. I can adapt. It's the older ones I'm afraid for. Many people may have to leave their homes—in country districts not only their homes, but their farms and villages. The Turks have said more than once that if they cannot have the whole island then it must be divided—equal shares for Greeks and Turks. There is bound to be disruption such as we have never experienced before."

"Well, you go carefully, and let's hope when I'm next back in Cyprus on a business trip we can see each other again."

"I hope so," she said, now smiling a little. "After all, we have much in common, in particular the secret of our very own private vendetta. Until I met you, Richard, and your determination gave me the strength I needed, I never thought I could kill someone. I won't say murder, because to me what we've done is nothing of the kind, merely justice, a punishment to fit the crime. Now I have helped in the killing of two men, and part of the ache I feel at your going is that I will be unable to kill the third—that you will have him all to yourself."

"Very selfish."

"You'd better go now, Richard. The best time for parting is when we are able to smile at each other and laugh a little at ourselves."

I nodded, grateful for the opportunity and for her resolute display of acceptance.

"Don't come down with me," I murmured. "I'd rather we said good-bye here. I've always hated partings. I like the break to be quick and clean."

She reached up on tiptoe and kissed my cheek. Her good-bye

129

came to me as a mere whisper. Then I was in the passage outside the flat and the door was closing behind me as I went down the stairs. The sound echoed throughout the building—final, definite.

Before I got into the car I looked up and was able to see her figure in shadow just inside the window, watching. I raised a hand and she did likewise. I turned my back on the block of flats and eased myself behind the steering wheel. Perhaps this last, indistinct view of her is my most enduring memory. Despite my hopes and words of assurance, I felt I would never see her again. To minimize any further risk to each other we had agreed not to correspond or get in touch in any way. There was to be no communication between us except for the brief message I had agreed to send to let her know of the death of Stephanides Tengerakis.

Our precautions were useless, totally unnecessary. Eventually they killed her, then came after me. Our Judas had been with us all the time, aboard the *Fontana Amorosa*. Had I been more alert I might have recognized the slight figure, lighting a cigarette, turning away behind a parked car as I drove away from the block of flats. I saw him, caught a glimpse of the face in profile, and thought for a moment I recognized that face, had seen it before; then as quickly as the thought had come to my mind I dismissed it entirely. It was only much later, when time and again I went over every single event I could recall, that this face in the shadows merged with the face of a deckhand on the ship. I'll never know who he was—a Tengerakis relative, perhaps, or a family friend. But somehow the Tengerakises must have pieced together the circumstances surrounding the brothers' separate deaths and found the link connecting Maria and myself. When, later, I was to learn that they had killed her, only then did I become fully aware of the power within a Mediterranean family, of the numbers of relatives who could be mustered to pursue a vendetta every bit as calculated and ruthless as the one I myself had initiated.

There were several hundred people waiting for flights to Britain when I arrived at Akrotiri. During the previous few days hundreds of wives and children of service personnel and British businessmen had been airlifted out. The evacuation had now established a routine, controlled with efficiency by harassed men and women of the RAF. A young Air Movements flight lieutenant told me that I would not have too long to wait for a seat aboard a VC-10. The initial rush seemed to be over, and space aboard aircraft was now being allocated in much the same fashion as if one were booking a flight with a civilian airline. My name was placed on a passenger list and I was given a boarding card stamped with a number. I dozed off in the Akrotiri departure lounge, surrounded by the noise of children playing together or crying, voices issuing official instructions over the public address system, droning conversation. When eventually I awoke to find an airman asking my name, then ticking it off on a sheaf of paper attached to a clipboard, I looked at my watch and saw it was twelve minutes past ten. The VC-10, every seat occupied, took off twenty minutes later. Beneath me for several minutes I could just see in the darkness the lights of Limassol, then the jet was climbing steeply and Cyprus was gone; Maria was gone. There was only the memory of two men dead and a future in which the death of the third was the most important objective of all.

≥ ≥ ≥

When I got back to England the first week was busy. There were masses of business paperwork to be read, initialed, and commented upon, files to be scrutinized, and decisions to be implemented in my office; and in the evenings I felt it only right that Felicity should have my undivided attention. The children were staying with friends, so we had only each other to consider. I love my wife, and apart from a couple of lapses, including the night I had made love to Maria aboard the *Fontana Amorosa,* I had remained faithful to her. I'm certainly attracted to other women and always have been, but somehow I've never availed myself of opportunities presented to me. As far as I know, Felicity has behaved in a similar fashion. She may have secrets, just as I have, but if she has, I'm content for them to remain a part of her innermost self. The strength of our love and relationship is such that I would not want to know these things, because throughout our years of marriage there has developed a re-

131

spect, a mutual understanding, that goes far beyond the bounds of possessive desire. Right from the start this harmony began to develop. It has linked our lives ever since.

All the same, by Tuesday of the second week after my return I was finding it increasingly difficult to return home from London each evening knowing that as yet I had made no attempt to find Stephanides Tengerakis. Before I left home that morning I told Felicity that I intended to stay in town to have dinner with a business colleague. I went into the room I use as my study and library and took from a drawer in my desk the trusted knife that had traveled with me to Cyprus and Greece. In its sheath against my left thigh it fitted snugly and unobtrusively beneath my business suit. My mind was made up.

I felt no trace of nervousness, merely a thrill of anticipation, a feeling that persisted and intensified throughout the day—in the train traveling to London, during the hours of conversation with colleagues and secretaries, on the telephone to various European cities—until, when I stepped out into the street shortly after six o'clock and mingled with the last of the evening rush-hour crowds, my body was in such a state of awareness that no force would have been capable of stopping what I intended to do.

In a way it was almost as if I were being transported through some drug-induced hallucination. All the time, people were around me by the hundreds on the pavements, in passages, and on the escalators of the underground system and on the tube trains. But I moved among them as if totally alone, seeing only one face in my mind, a face that was a younger version of the two brothers I had already killed, a face which, although I had never seen it, I had come to visualize and loathe.

As I look back now, there is something frightening about the way my mind was totally possessed that day by the desire to kill. In a way, I suppose it could be described as a form of temporary insanity. But to be insane one has to lose all reason; the mind must divorce itself from the actions of the body. And my mind was acting in concert with my body as I emerged from Gloucester Road underground station and walked along Cromwell Road toward the address

Maria had given me; my reason was crystal clear, and my nerves and muscles were under control, honed to such intensity that I seemed to move like a shadow through a background of total anonymity.

≥ ≥ ≥

The place was in a cul-de-sac, a flat in a five-story terraced house, its period charm still visible beneath the cracked and peeling stucco. To the right of the entrance beneath a flaking portico were steps leading to the basement. A tiny courtyard, shielded from the street by a high wall topped by tall black railings, lay in front of a red door alongside which was a narrow sash window painted white and red.

I glanced at the names of the residents scrawled in ink on pieces of white card inserted in slots alongside the various bells. Judging by the number of names, some of the flats seemed to be occupied by several people of both sexes, but only one name was on the card belonging to the basement—S. Tengerakis. There was no bell. That was beside the door at the foot of the eight worn steps. I descended quickly, already framing the first words of the conversation that would, without difficulty, I hoped, gain me entrance to the flat.

I pressed the bell. It buzzed with a shrill echo, and somehow the hollow sound told me there was no one inside to hear it. I pressed it again three times in rapid succession, stabbing my finger at the narrow white button as the first traces of frustration crept over me. I listened for almost a minute, then went to the window and pressed my face against the glass. But my head and shoulders obscured the upper panes, and all I could see was an inner gloom and the vague reflection of my features staring back at me.

I was crouched in this fashion when I heard the main door to the house opening and closing. Hastily I straightened up and turned my head. A young woman was standing at the top of the steps. She was tall and slim, and despite the frown on her face there was a hint of warmth in her voice when she said, "You won't find him in at this time, love. He'll have gone to the club by now."

"The club? I don't understand."

She flicked her shoulder-length hair and moved her legs so that I

133

heard her nylons rustling as they pressed against each other. She was around twenty or twenty-one, with clear, fresh skin. In the evening sunlight her body stood out clear-cut and perfect against the background of grime and neglect.

"You are a friend of his, I suppose?" she asked sharply.

"Oh, yes," I replied without thinking. "I've met him on several occasions."

She stared at me; this time there was a frank, appraising quality in her expression.

"Then how come you don't know about the club? He's a barman there."

I shrugged my shoulders, but thought it prudent not to reply. I hoped she would accept this casual gesture. She did.

"I'm sorry, love," she said. "I just thought you'd met him there, that's all. Got to know him better after that. Still, I suppose he does have other friends from those he keeps bringing back from the club. God knows there's enough of them. Up to all the bleedin' hours they are some nights. And the records he plays—I sometimes think I'll scream if I'm forced to listen to any more Greek music, I really do. I should know. I live right above."

She gestured with her head in the direction of the windows above the basement flat. At the same time she laughed softly, then said, "Don't mind me. I'm not complaining, not really. I mind my own business. He seems a nice enough bloke and I'll give you this, he is good looking. He's entitled to his fun. God knows there's little enough of it in this country. Folks are entitled to do what they please, that's what I say. I like a laugh and a giggle myself, and loud music when I'm entertaining the right company. So I suppose me and him are quits when it comes to noise and enjoying ourselves."

I hadn't moved since she'd first spoken to me, hoping that my face would be too indistinct for her to remember, should she ever be called upon to do so, in the pool of shadow shrouding the inner part of the basement courtyard. Her shoes scraped on the flagstones as she started to move toward the pavement.

"I must dash, else I'll be late for my date. Hope you find him."

"The club," I said. "Where is it?"

134

She halted, swinging around by taking hold of the railings, her body swaying from side to side.

"Oh, yes—Sandy's in Hogarth Place, just off the Earls Court Road. It's not far. Eight, perhaps ten minutes' walk. Down here"—she gestured with one hand—"then turn left. Two—no, three streets along, left again. It's about fifty yards up on the right."

She giggled. "You can't miss it. It's slap bang between a fancy restaurant and a sex shop."

"Thanks."

"Don't mention it. Have fun. I will."

She waved, then disappeared onto the pavement. I stayed in the courtyard for almost a minute, listening to the fading sounds of her footsteps. When I climbed the steps and looked along the street she was turning the corner going toward the right. I hesitated briefly, then started to walk slowly away from the house.

For several minutes I walked aimlessly, trying to decide what I should do, whether or not I should wait, then return later to the flat in hopes he would be there; whether I should simply go home and try again some other time, perhaps the following day; whether I should go to the club, have a drink, if possible observe him at close quarters, then decide what to do and when to do it.

My deliberation was meaningless. I had absorbed too much tension during the day, been held too firmly in the grip of anticipation, for me to abandon my mission that evening. Somehow, as I wandered along the pavements, halting now and then to gaze vacantly into shop windows, I sensed it was useless even to think of changing my plans. It had to be done. It had to be done now. I went to Sandy's Club, finding it easily, thanks to the girl's directions.

⩾ ⩾ ⩾

I went through the doorway and climbed a flight of stairs to a carpeted reception area bathed in a warm orange glow from lights fastened to the paneled walls. Hanging between the lights were framed stills from early Hollywood movies and here and there larger photographs, also framed, of handsome youths and young men, some of whom wore nothing but a coy, beguiling smile. On one side was a

135

cloakroom with several racks for hanging coats and in front of it a broad, polished table behind which sat a slender, blond youth reading a magazine. The faint sound of music, a slow, mournful New Orleans number played on a trumpet, drifted from behind a long velvet curtain suspended from a shining brass rail. I halted in front of the youth. He laid down the magazine and looked up smiling; it was a fresh, open face.

"May I see your membership card, sir?" he said. There was a faint trace of Cockney in the accent.

I hesitated momentarily, aware that behind the youth a burly, moustached figure was scrutinizing me from the depths of the cloakroom. There was something unnerving in the way his eyes seemed fixed on my face. I stared back at him, then hurriedly looked away.

"I'm not a member. Sorry, does it matter?"

The youth smiled again, showing neat, white teeth.

"No, not really." He glanced at me casually, pursing his lips a little. The cursory inspection seemed to satisfy him that on the surface at least I didn't look like a troublemaker. His right hand reached for a pen, and with his left he pulled a card from a box at the front of the table. "Mind you, it'll cost you as a casual visitor—a temporary member is how we describe it. If you're going to become a regular patron you'd be better to take full membership. That's twenty pounds for a year."

Two men came up the stairs and went past me. One was sober-suited, gray-haired, in his mid-fifties, with a prosperous appearance. His companion was small and dark haired, slim, twentyish, casually dressed. The older man's right arm was fastened protectively around the other's waist. The youth behind the table nodded, and they both smiled at him before disappearing into the room behind the curtain. A last lingering high note from the trumpet hung in the air, then came silence, broken only by muffled clapping.

"I'll think about it," I said. "How much for tonight?"

"Two pounds. That gives you temporary membership for a week. All right?"

I nodded, feeling inside my jacket for my wallet.

"Your name?"

136

I replied immediately, the false name coming easily from my tongue as if all the time I had planned to use it.

"Armstrong. John Armstrong."

He wrote the name on the card, took the two pound notes from me, and slid them into a drawer at his side. He then made an entry in an open ledger and got to his feet, sliding the ledger around in front of me.

"Please sign this, sir."

I scrawled "John Armstrong" next to the place where he had printed the name and written the words *temporary member*. He glanced at the page as I signed, then handed me the card.

"Right, John, welcome to Sandy's Club. Go right ahead. In the room behind the curtain there's a dance floor and bar. There's another smaller bar just off that with a stairway leading to the restaurant you must have seen on your way in. We own that as well. One part for the general public, another reserved for club members. You'll get a decent meal if you want something to eat. Anyhow, enjoy yourself. It's a bit early yet, but things usually liven up a little later in the evening. There's more talent around then—and of course there's the band. But at the moment Jackie Weston's in there playing solo trumpet. He's smashing—super bloke, great musician."

"Thanks," I said, moving toward the doorway. He was at my side, reaching for the curtain.

"In town on business?" he asked. I saw him glance at my clothes. I was suddenly aware of my conventional city attire, the pin-striped suit—*businessman* was stamped all over me.

"Yes—yes, that's right," I replied. "Just for a couple of days—attending a conference."

He grinned, eyes flashing.

"I thought as much. I've worked here for a few months now. On duty most evenings. It's just that I didn't recall ever having seen you here before. And most blokes who come here usually come back."

"Well, this is my first night. A friend recommended your club to me."

He looked pleased. The permanent smile widened. I liked his

137

charm, his spontaneous good nature. There was nothing ingratiating or offhand in his behavior. Open sincerity was something rare in such establishments.

"Good," he said. "Then enjoy yourself. You've come to a good place. Sandy's Club has no riffraff. The members are all ages—and inclinations. On the whole, they're a good bunch."

He pulled aside the curtain. When I was through the doorway I heard him say, "'Bye for now, John," then there was a swishing sound as the velvet material slid along behind me. On a stage in the far corner a black man in his late twenties was putting a trumpet to his lips. He started to play slowly and softly at first, the blues number growing in strength and intensity as I moved across the floor toward a long bar counter stretching the full length of one wall.

There were several figures seated on stools in front of the counter, and as my eyes grew accustomed to the subdued lighting I saw a number of other men, couples and singles, sitting around small tables placed in a semicircle beside an area reserved for dancing. Behind the bar there were two figures, a man of about forty checking the money in the drawer of the cash register and a younger man in his early twenties with a sullen, handsome face framed by thick black hair, emptying a bottle of lager into a glass.

I had seen enough in Cyprus and Greece to dispel any further doubts. I had found Stephanides Tengerakis.

≫ ≫ ≫ **7**

⩾ ⩾ ⩾

Stephanides Tengerakis had been aware for almost an hour that Richard was watching him. As yet the Greek Cypriot had not served him a drink, but Stephanides realized that this new patron of Sandy's had already downed several whiskies poured by Harry, his colleague. He decided that the next time the man approached the bar he would serve him; he looked prosperous. The suit was a trifle formal for the middle of the evening in this establishment, but at least it hinted of money. It helped to dispel any doubts on that score. And, thought Stephanides, this newcomer wasn't bad looking: thirtyish, he'd say, stockily built, well muscled, not fat. That would be an added bonus. He was pleased.

Not that Stephanides worried too much about his clients' physical appearance. It was the money that was important, the ability of whomever he went with to reward him handsomely. After all, he always made sure they enjoyed themselves. And they did. Several were now customers on a regular basis. Their money was better than the usual. They seemed willing to pay extra for the regular pleasure of his company.

Stephanides had come to London to make money. Already he was succeeding beyond his wildest dreams. His wages as a barman at the club did not amount to much, but simply being here opened the door to greater earnings, the chance to accumulate the sort of wealth that, when he returned to Cyprus, would make that bitch Maria appreciate him. His determination to marry her was stronger than ever. Love had no part in his decision. He'd never loved her, but his father had been promised by her father that she would be married to Stephanides, and he and his father wanted the land belonging to the Pierides family. To Stephanides land meant power. Land plus money promised great power.

In the village where they had grown up together he'd always thought of her as attractive. But he didn't love her and didn't want her love. Stephanides would expect—would demand—her obedience and submission, and she would bear his children. She would serve his purpose, just as the men to whom he offered his body were serving his purpose by providing him with the funds to make his eventual return a triumphant one.

He had been in London for only a matter of months and already his bank account held over two hundred pounds. The rent for his flat was paid by a company executive who came to the city twice a month and stayed for a couple of nights on both occasions. To Stephanides it was a fair return. He knew the man thought so. Stephanides even liked some of the men, and not just the younger ones, in his circle of clients. Sometimes he laughed to himself when he thought about what he was doing—selling his body to men so that a woman's body could become his.

It flattered him that his wiry, slender frame and his mop of shining black hair could have such appeal. He'd never thought about his attractiveness to men until two days after his arrival, when he had been drinking in a Soho pub and a man had propositioned him. The idea had excited him, and in the furnished room that had been his first lodging in the city he had stripped off his clothes in front of the stranger and heard him say, "Oh, boy—you're a stunner. You could make a small fortune with that sort of body." In that moment, and seconds later as he felt the stranger's arms close around his back, Stephanides had seen the path he should follow.

He hadn't charged anything that night. In a way he'd felt grateful

142

to the man for planting the idea in his mind. But the following evening, without even making an obvious gesture, he'd sat in the same pub and within minutes a man was at his side offering him a cigarette. An hour later he was asking for ten pounds from the man even before either of them had unfastened a shirt button. And the man gave him the money—willingly.

From then on Stephanides had worked hard to perfect a graceful technique, using hitherto undiscovered powers of flattery and charm. The clients had materialized one after the other, wealthier clients, then the barman's job at Sandy's Club and the small flat within easy reach. He had everything now, everything except the fortune he intended to accumulate, and that was growing every day. And Maria. Someday she would be his. And the land. One day. Then the feeling of power, invincibility, all would be his. When that happened his satisfaction would be complete.

In London Stephanides' life had run smoothly. There had been a few occasions when his quick temper had flared and his intense, pathological rage, which always arose when someone or something threatened his superiority, had all but overwhelmed him. He had been aware of this trait in his character since boyhood days and had learned to use it to his advantage to obtain what he wanted. When with Andreas and Nicos he'd been torturing the young English officer, the feeling of anger raging inside him had been different, however; on that occasion it had almost blinded him, so great had been his hatred of the man and his contempt for Maria.

When he'd been first to take the revolver and place it against the man's head, to Stephanides the squeezing of the trigger could well have been a moment of sexual release. The body on its knees slumping forward, the sight of the blood, and the empty cry from the dying man's throat had all stimulated such excitement within him that ever since Stephanides had lived with a feeling of invincibility; he seemed always on the brink of an opportunity to put it to the test once again.

Only one client had ever argued about the amount Stephanides had asked for his services. At first the Greek Cypriot had looked at him coldly, but even this had failed to stop the man's protests.

143

Within seconds Stephanides had crossed the room to fling himself across the naked figure. His hands were around the man's throat before the other realized what was happening, fingers squeezing, nails gouging, pushing the head up, twisting the neck. Just as abruptly he had stopped, let go, and straightened up, remaining astride the struggling figure.

"Pay now, what I ask. Or I'll kill you."

That was all he had said. And when he'd released him the man had paid, rubbing his throat with one hand, keeping his distance from the handsome, brooding figure circling around him in the room, watching him constantly like a cat taunting its prey.

From then on Stephanides had insisted on cash first, pleasure later. It saved arguments, prevented trouble. Killing someone in Cyprus or, as he had done as a schoolboy, gathering information about those his brothers wanted to kill, had involved little risk. Here in London it would not be such an easy matter. The risks were too great. And no amount of pleasure was worth the risk of detection.

≽ ≽ ≽

The trumpeter had now been joined by several other musicians to form a jazz combo. Several couples danced in the center of the floor, swaying in time to the slow beat of the music. There were several young men in drag, a feminine beauty to their faces and figures even without the make-up and dresses they wore so well. But for the most part, the majority of the patrons were conventional looking. There were numerous middle-aged men and many younger ones, wearing suits or dressed casually in sweaters and jeans. Here and there in the crowd was the occasional touch of the bizarre: a heavy medallion worn proudly on a chest bared by a shirt slashed open to the waist, glittering earrings, a head of hair dyed in two shades, an aging face with mascara deftly applied. Such figures were in the minority. In the main the crowd was no more than a fair cross-section of society, their very normality signified by accents and appearances and conventional behavior. There were also several women in the room, but they sat together ignoring the men, eyes on each other.

144

Now that the bar was crowded there were waiters serving drinks to those seated at the tables: five young men in red shirts to match the decor and upholstery, tight white trousers, and black-and-white shoes. Stephanides smiled at one of them as he placed a number of drinks on a tray. The waiter winked in return, then carried it away, weaving expertly among the dancers. As Stephanides reached for several dirty glasses to wash at the sink beneath the counter, he saw Richard talking to a young man wearing horn-rimmed glasses. The two were laughing together, then as Richard shook his head the younger man shrugged his shoulders and walked over to another table.

At once Stephanides felt Richard's eyes fall on him yet again. This time he boldly returned the stare, holding the gaze across the smoke-filled room. He could see Richard rising to his feet. He was hidden for several seconds by a couple on the dance floor, then when the way was clear Stephanides saw him coming toward the bar. He felt a glow of excitement deep in the pit of his stomach.

He was perfectly aware of his good looks and the effect they had on many of the club's patrons. This was why things had been so easy for him. But it had been some time since a pair of eyes had been fastened on him so frankly and with such persistent candor. In that case, if the man wanted him so much, Stephanides expected he would be willing to pay more than handsomely for the opportunity.

Richard passed behind the crowded bar stools. He nodded, inclining his head slightly to let Stephanides know he was going to the far end of the bar. There was an empty space between a pillar there and the wall. Stephanides smiled, dipping his head to acknowledge the glance; then, ignoring a voice behind him requesting two double whiskies, he walked quickly to his new client, who was positioning himself against the counter.

When Stephanides was close he saw the man running his eyes over him—"assessing the goods," was how Stephanides described such a look. He wriggled his hips a little, then flicked his head so that his hair bobbed. He was puzzled by the lack of warmth in the man's smile. Now that they were only a few feet apart he could see that the same intense stare was there, but the eyes were cold, like

145

steel, and in the set of the features there was a challenging, almost defiant expression.

"You are Stephanides Tengerakis?" Richard asked.

For an instant the smile vanished from the Greek Cypriot's face, the expression being replaced by one of complete surprise. It was not so much that the man knew his name; many of the club's members knew it and he assumed the man had obtained it from one of them. No, it was the definite, authoritative tone of the man's voice, as if he wanted to make certain there was no mistake. Stephanides nodded, moistening his lips with the tip of his tongue.

"Yes," he replied. "Yes, I am. Friends call me Stephan." He laughed nervously. "It's shorter, much easier to say. But how did you know me?"

Richard's stare was expressionless for a moment, then, knowing what he had to do, knowing that he must for the moment restrain his feelings, curb the hate within him, he relaxed a little. He forced a smile and said, "A mutual acquaintance told me about you, Stephan; someone who knows you well. I wanted to ask if you're free later on. I want to talk to you."

Stephanides smiled once again, his self-assurance returning. He realized that the man was not used to such encounters, had not yet overcome the mental barrier against buying sexual pleasure. Certainly in a club such as Sandy's no one had any need to feel inhibited.

"Sure," he replied. "I'll be glad to. You're in luck, I finish early tonight." He glanced at his wristwatch. "In an hour's time—at half past nine."

Their eyes met. Behind their enigmatic expressions each was alone with his thoughts of how the next few hours would be.

≥ ≥ ≥

Richard left the club a few minutes ahead of the Greek Cypriot. Overhead it was almost dark and the street lighting was on. He gazed for several minutes into the windows of the sex shop with their displays of magazines and invitations to step inside to view the

146

range of aids to sexual harmony. Loud pop music boomed through the open doorway, and he watched several people entering and leaving before Stephanides touched him on the arm and indicated he was ready to go.

"My flat is very close to here," he said. "Do you want to go there, or to your own place?"

"Yours will do," Richard replied, suddenly struck by the incongruity of the evening he had spent. Snippets of conversation overheard in the bar and the way the Greek Cypriot had returned his own uncompromising stare had given him the idea. When at the bar he had spoken his first words to Stephanides he had known his assumptions were correct, that the Greek Cypriot's eye for the benefits of prostitution was more attentive than his sense of his duties as a barman. Richard had enjoyed acting the role that was required of him. But now, in the street, walking toward the cul-de-sac, he felt no overwhelming hatred of the young man alongside him.

Instead, to his surprise, he had become curiously detached, viewing the act of killing with almost impersonal aloofness as if, instead of pursuing a personal revenge, he had been hired to do a necessary duty, had become a private assassin to compensate for someone else's loss. The hate was still there, deep within him, the urge to avenge as strong-rooted as ever. But now in his brain there was no ferment of emotion. His mind was cool, razor sharp; now that he was so close to his quarry, so close that he could touch him if he wished, he was guided by the absolute instinct of the calculating killer. At any other time the thought might have frightened him. Now there was no fear, merely an awareness of his new identity.

There was no one in front of the house when they descended the steps and entered the flat. After shutting the front door, Stephanides led him along a narrow passage and into the room that overlooked the courtyard. It was obviously used as a sitting room. There were a couple of armchairs and a television set in one corner. A pile of magazines spilled onto the floor from a low table beneath the window; a dirty glass stood among some china ornaments on a sideboard. On a table in the center of the room a paperback book lay

147

open on top of a crumpled shirt. Stephanides drew the curtains and switched on a standard lamp that stood beside a small two-bar electric fire.

Richard felt a tightening sensation in the muscles at the back of his neck; a dull pounding came from his heart. On his earlier visit he had intended to use the knife. It would have been easy then. Now there were a number of people who would at least be able to describe him, to connect him with the Greek Cypriot. The method of death must appear, to those who would find the body, to be either an accident or suicide.

Stephanides went to the sideboard. He looked over his shoulder, smiling a little, mistaking the expression of deep thought on Richard's face for one of shy reticence.

"Come on, relax. Would you like a drink? I have some sherry—whisky, too."

Richard nodded. "A whisky."

The Greek Cypriot poured two measures of whisky, then carried the glasses across the room. Their fingers touched as Richard accepted his glass. Stephanides smiled.

"What about water?"

"No, thanks. I can take it neat."

Stephanides raised his glass, then touched it lightly against Richard's.

"A toast to us." He laughed. "I don't know your name."

"John."

"But John who?"

"Just John."

The Greek Cypriot eyed him across the rim of his upraised glass.

"I think you're a little nervous, John. You've no need to be. I enjoy what I do. I am the soul of discretion. There is no need for false names or to be afraid of telling me things. I do this for the money. I don't blackmail any of my clients. Why should I? I want them to come back for more."

Richard sipped the whisky, a rough, badly matured blend that made his throat burn. An idea had come into his mind, an idea

148

which in the circumstances should be so easy to realize that merely to think about it brought an anticipatory glow to his body. "Make him suffer," Maria had said.

"I haven't done much of this sort of thing," he said.

Stephanides put down his empty glass and took hold of Richard's free hand. Richard felt himself go tense, wanting to lash out, but he managed to control himself. Now was not the moment to act rashly.

"You have not had to pay for it before," said Stephanides, stroking his hand, fingers lightly caressing fingers. "Am I right?"

Richard nodded, draining his own whisky, the warmth in the pit of his stomach now a mixture of spirits and sharpened excitement. He had only to wait just a little longer.

"Then I will make it easy for you, John. I charge fifteen pounds for—how shall I put it?—for a short time together. If you want to stay longer, all night perhaps, then it is more, say thirty pounds. Payable in advance."

Richard jerked his hand away and reached into his jacket. He extracted six five-pound notes and placed them on the table. Stephanides picked them up, then opened a drawer in the sideboard and slipped them inside. When the drawer was shut he turned and stood for several seconds leaning against the sideboard, unbuttoning his shirt.

"I thought somehow you were the type who might want to stay all night," he said. "The bedroom is through there." He pointed to the open doorway leading into the passage.

Richard heard his voice, steady and controlled, saying, "Can you run a bath?"

For a moment Stephanides stopped, half out of the shirt. Then he dropped the garment to the floor and rubbed his hands across his bare chest. A frown creased his face; his full lips were pursed.

"A bath? There is no need. I may not be British, but I am perfectly clean. I have never been asked to take a bath before."

Aware of the mounting anger in the Greek Cypriot's voice but amused by the confusion caused by what to him had seemed like a casual remark, Richard went quickly across the room. He placed his

149

hands on Stephanides' shoulders. His fingers wanted to squeeze the slender throat, lock around the unprotected neck. Instead they stroked the skin, soothing the other's anger.

"No, Stephan," he said. "You misunderstand me. I'm not suggesting you have a bath. I meant that we could have a bath— together. I like it that way. It can be fun."

Stephanides started to laugh, and inwardly Richard breathed a sigh of relief. The Greek Cypriot patted his cheek, then slipped from his grasp.

"Sure, sure," he said. "I think the water is hot enough. I have a feeling we are going to enjoy ourselves. At least you have some novel ideas—different tastes. It makes a change. Come."

He beckoned and Richard followed him into the passage. The bedroom door was partly open. The Greek Cypriot switched on the light and drew a pair of curtains across the window.

"Leave your clothes in here. The bathroom is there." He pointed to the far end of the passage. "I will run the water. Come through when you are ready."

Richard decided to strip down to his briefs. There was no point in getting his clothing wet. What he had to do might be messy. On the other hand, he didn't know for sure. All he had to go on was what he had read in newspapers when similar accidents had occurred. From these he knew well enough the effect was instantaneous, and deadly. But then the hapless victims of such accidents had died unaware it was about to happen. He knew he could make Stephanides suffer, because for several moments Stephanides would absorb what he was about to do and why he was doing it. Richard would make sure of that.

From the bathroom he heard the sound of gushing water and Stephanides' whistling, then, moments later, his voice calling, "John." Richard walked slowly toward the bathroom, tension ebbing a little when he saw an electrical socket in the baseboard in the passage close to the bathroom door. He looked into the bathroom and caught sight of the Greek Cypriot amid the swirling steam, naked, with one foot in the water testing the temperature and the other still on the floor.

150

"It is fine," he said, turning to look at Richard. He took the foot out of the bath and stood facing him, hands resting on his narrow hips, a puddle of water forming on the floor. For a moment Richard stared at the body flaunting itself in front of him: the overhandsome face, the large lips, the neat lines of chest and hips, the flat stomach, the long, firmly muscled legs. He found it hard to believe that evil, such black evil, could exist within such near perfection.

"You are modest," said Stephanides, pointing to his briefs.

Richard looked down for a moment, then laughed and glanced around the room. Rivulets of condensation were streaming down the walls, on the mirror, the frosted glass of the window.

"Yes," he replied. "Time enough yet." He wriggled his shoulders a little, feigning cold.

"It's still a bit chilly in here. Don't you have a heater?"

"I don't feel cold. Anyway, you will be warm in the bath with me. When I want any heat I plug in a heater out there in the passage and bring it in here."

"That's very dangerous," said Richard, relishing the moment of boldness.

The Greek Cypriot shrugged his shoulders. The edges of his long hair were curling in the damp atmosphere.

"I take care. But bring the heater through from the sitting room if you wish. I don't mind. While you are doing that I'll get into the bath."

"Yes, do that," murmured Richard as he turned away to walk back along the passage. He could hear the sound of water splashing and slopping in the bath. From the bedroom he collected his handkerchief and then, in the sitting room, placed it over the plug, which he pulled from the power socket. Transferring the handkerchief to the handle, he lifted the heater, pleased by the long length of the cord. As he left the room he noticed a small transistor radio lying on its side beside one of the chairs. A second idea came to him; there could well be some noise. He went softly along the passage and quietly placed the heater on the floor. Inside the bathroom Stephanides was whistling again. Returning to the sitting room, Richard used the handkerchief to lift the radio. He flicked the switch

151

and adjusted the waveband until he heard pop music from one of the commercial stations. He turned up the volume; the song and its accompanying rhythm of guitars and drums emerged in a thin jangle that hurt his eardrums. He went toward the bathroom and put the radio on the floor alongside the heater.

He heard Stephanides call, "I like that song. It's a great hit at the moment."

Richard did not reply. He put the plug into the socket and switched on the heater. Within seconds both bars of it started to glow. He could hear the movements of water in the bath and the Greek Cypriot humming the tune of the song now blaring from the radio. The head of the bath with the faucets was directly behind the partly open door. There was a narrow ledge between them and the wall. The cord would have to be sufficiently long to go completely around the edge of the door. He had no way of testing, not now. He was committed. Some things would have to be left to chance.

Richard took hold of the handle of the heater and carried it at waist level into the bathroom. Stephanides was leaning against the far end of the bathtub, his feet pointing toward the faucets. The water partially covered his body. He was lazily stroking his chest with a bar of soap. Foam clung to the dark hairs on his chest and around his nipples. He sighed and raised one leg, stretching out.

"This is good," he said. "You have given me ideas for the future. I can hardly wait——"

"There will be no future," said Richard, staring down at the reclining figure. "Not for you."

≥ ≥ ≥

For a moment Stephanides stared up in blank amazement, struck by the coldness in Richard's voice. He eyed the glowing heater that the man held in front of him while his mind tried to absorb what the new client had said. As his mind and vision aligned themselves, the slow horror of it crept over his limp, relaxed body. He started to ease himself up against the bathtub.

"Stay quite still. Exactly as you are. If you move one inch I'll dump this thing right on top of you."

152

Richard saw the color drain from the Greek Cypriot's face, watched as the eyes widened, fear and desperation enlarging the pupils until the face stared at him transfixed, paralyzed by a dawning realization of total helplessness.

"But why?"

The voice emerged as a dry croak. Outside the room the radio emitted a raucous jangle of sound. The music finished and a woman was talking on the telephone to the disc jockey in the studio. She was asking for help in dealing with her alcoholic husband. "It'll kill him, it really will. It'll be the death of me if this drinking of his goes on for much longer." The disc jockey's smooth accent droned on, soothing her, offering advice. Then another record started to play.

"But why?"

Suddenly Richard was aware of the repeated question.

"Because you killed my brother. Tortured and killed him. Don't tell me you've forgotten—or is killing such second nature to you that you forget about it the moment it's done?"

At first Stephanides appeared not to have heard, then within seconds the full shock took hold of him. He tried to raise his arms, holding them out in front of his body as if in some way they would protect him against the inevitable.

"The UN officer? You are his brother? You are Barker? John Barker?"

The words were a whisper of incredulity.

Richard nodded, smiling a little, starting to relish his domination, the exquisite feeling of power. The hate was rising fast in him now, flooding over. He heard Maria's words, "Make him suffer," repeated again and again until his head throbbed.

"Correct in almost every aspect," he said. "Except that my name is Richard. I made up the other one."

Richard edged closer to the head of the bath. There were still several feet of cord to spare. It would be long enough. Stephanides drew in his legs, pulling them up against the rest of his body, arms outstretched, huddling into the corner, water slopping and eddying.

"I've seen Maria Pierides," Richard said. "She told me what you had done, you and your brothers. Once—a long time ago—I thought every man had the right to life despite any abominable crimes he might have committed. My views changed gradually over the years. They changed completely when I heard how you tortured and executed my brother Jonathan. Murdered him without mercy. You unspeakable bastard. I've waited some time for this. You were left to the end. At the time, it was more convenient to deal with your brothers. They——"

"You have killed them too?"

"Yes. Hadn't you heard?"

"No."

"Then let me be the first to give you the news. Now it's your turn. Even now I'm not convinced that your death in this way isn't too good for you. It's too quick."

Stephanides stared hypnotically at Richard's hands grasping the handle of the heater. But despite his fear he still retained a measure of pride, pride that would prevent him from pleading for his life. Even in the final moments, as he waited for the split second that might catch Richard unawares, he was determined to deny the Englishman the satisfaction of hearing him ask for a mercy he knew could never be his. It was obvious that this was Richard's intention. He was holding the heater directly above the bath, pulling it back toward his body, moving it forward, backward, forward, watching him all the time.

Richard lifted the heater even higher, holding it now in one hand. He saw the Greek Cypriot's shoulder muscles go tense, then Stephanides was pushing himself up against the bathtub, sliding up the wall, one foot almost on a level with the rim of the tub. Richard released the heater. At the same time he jumped back. Stephanides was slewed to one side, back against the wall, left leg dangling over the bathtub, right leg still in the water from knee to foot.

The heater bumped against the side of the bathtub, then plunged into the water. For several seconds the bathroom became a turmoil of music blaring from the radio, a hissing, a thump like a distant explosion, several flashes of vivid blue light, a short scream, sharp and high pitched, and splashing and slopping as the body thrashed in the water, arms and legs flailing. There was smoke and steam and a sound like frying fat.

154

When Richard could see clearly again, the Greek Cypriot's body was slumped in the bath in a sitting position, arms forward, head dropping against the chest. He watched for several minutes, bending forward to look at the chest, taking care not to touch the body or any part of the tub. There was no pulsation on the skin over the heart. There was a faint smell of burning, a mixture of singed flesh, where a foot had jerked forward to touch the heater, and rubber.

Now that it was over and all the killings were accomplished, Richard felt a feeling of emptiness inside him, as if he had awakened from a dream. There was no sense of achievement, only a gnawing uneasiness that made him want to get away as quickly as possible.

≥ ≥ ≥

Richard went to the bedroom and dressed hurriedly. In the sitting room he extracted from the drawer in the sideboard the money he had given Stephanides and replaced it in his wallet. He took the whisky glasses into the kitchen and washed them under the faucet. When he had finished he dried them with his handkerchief, then wiped the handle of the faucet. He put the glasses into the sideboard beside the bottles.

In the passage he hesitated for a moment, trying to make up his mind what to do about the radio. He decided to leave it on. As he cautiously opened the door and let himself out, he could hear the disc jockey in conversation with a man who wanted advice on feeding a tame fox he was keeping in a suburban backyard. "Well, Jack, you have a problem there, you really have," drawled the bland voice, then the door was shut and Richard was in the courtyard, pushing the handkerchief into his trouser pocket.

He was just about to climb the steps when the entrance door to the flats opened. A beam of light lanced across the stonework above his head. He pressed his body into the pool of shadow against the wall of the house. The door slammed shut and footsteps went past, then faded away on the pavement. Turning his head, he could see the street beyond the railings; he was suddenly aware of his vulnerability to detection.

He mounted the steps two at a time and was on the pavement in

155

several easy bounds. Farther down the street he could see the figure of a young man, the one who had come from the house, passing beneath an overhead light. He walked slowly after him, and then the figure turned the corner and was lost from view.

Richard did not go to the nearest underground station, which he guessed would be Earls Court, but walked for some time along main streets and narrow lanes, through crescents and tree-lined squares, at times not sure what direction he was taking, aware only of the need to be alone. At South Kensington underground station he bought a ticket from a machine, then went down the escalator toward the platform. There were few people about; a couple stood near him and discussed a concert they'd just attended in the Albert Hall. He grew tired of listening to the woman expound on the solo violinist's "lovely timbre" in some concerto and moved away to a spot on his own near one end of the platform. Five minutes later a tube train appeared. As his carriage pulled away from the platform and entered the tunnel he felt some of the tension drain out of him. He even managed to smile to himself as he felt the pressure of the knife in its sheath against his thigh—the knife he had planned to use against each brother but had not once been stained with their blood.

When he reached the main-line station at Waterloo there were still several trains listed on the departure board which he could use to get home. He caught the first of them with only a couple of minutes to spare. He had a compartment to himself.

Halfway through his journey he heard himself saying aloud, "It's all over now. You're going home. Relax."

He tried to sleep, but each time he closed his eyes they came alive almost at once. He was forced to stare aimlessly around the compartment, seeing in the windows the reflection of his strained face. And somewhere in the distance, as if imprinted on the darkness of the passing landscape, were images of three faces, fading and spiraling away, plucked from his grasp into a void, to haunt him far beyond his reach.

156

≥≥≥ **8**

≥ ≥ ≥

The memory of my vendetta against the Tengerakis brothers lingered on in the following months as I gradually returned to a normal life centered around business and family. On the anniversary of Jonathan's death I was reminded of them again and of Maria somewhere in the divided island that was Cyprus since the crushing Turkish invasion the previous year.

I had heard nothing from Maria since I had left Cyprus, and apart from a short, unsigned note couched in the vaguest terms, which I'd sent to inform her that Stephanides had been killed, I had made no further contact with her. This was as we had agreed. It was hard but necessary. I thought too of Captain Stavros aboard his beloved *Fontana Amorosa*. Was he still sailing between Cyprus and Greece? At least now, with the reign of the colonels at an end and democracy once again controlling Greece, he would be able to play his Theodorakis records whenever he pleased.

All the same, time and routine had healed the scars in my mind. Although there were moments when I marveled at my accomplishment in surviving not only unscathed but undetected, the events of the past, awful though they may have been, seeped into my subconscious, no longer dominating my life. I had no great difficulty living with the memory of what I had done. I simply did my best to forget about it. Nature took care of the rest.

It was a couple of months later, in April, almost a year to the day since I had begun to plan my mission of vengeance, when the letter arrived from Cyprus. As soon as I slit open the envelope and withdrew the contents, I knew the vendetta was still alive, but this time in reverse. There was a folded piece of note paper, blank except for the letter T printed crudely in red ink. Fastened to the page was a clipping that I presumed came from one of the Cypriot newspapers.

> The body of a Limassol schoolteacher, Miss Maria Pierides, was found yesterday at the foot of a cliff close to the site of the Curium amphitheatre. Police believe that she slipped and fell to her death while engaged on an archaeological survey of the area for use in a school project.

The date of her death had been inserted at the side in the same red ink. The newspaper clipping was one month old.

For the first few minutes my thoughts were centered on Maria as I tried to absorb the shock of the news of her death—her murder. I tried desperately to find the link the family had discovered binding Maria to me and implicating us both in the killing of the three brothers, the link that had once again set in motion a thirst for revenge. Then, with the sudden onset of pain, I began to know the true meaning of fear, a fear unlike anything I had ever experienced. It was a crawling, gnawing feeling of apprehension which from that moment on caused me to equate every situation, no matter how innocent, with danger. This state persisted for several weeks, fraying my nerves as I waited for some further sign that they were close, some action that would bring me face to face with the deadly reality of it all.

For some reason, once it came, when I walked from my house and found Dodo, our pet donkey, with his throat cut in the paddock—and later when the shot was fired at my car in the lane and the tires were slashed—my fear eased a little. I was no longer terrified that something might happen. The fear and anxiety still

160

continued to haunt me, but now that they were closer and had made their move—the nameless, faceless beings who were part of the Tengerakis dynasty—I felt better able to come to terms with their vendetta, to face them and pit my wits against theirs.

Two nights after Felicity and the boys left for Spain, an old barn at the edge of a field not far from the house was set afire. I awoke about three in the morning, instinctively aware that something was wrong, unable in the first minute or so to react because of the deep sleep from which I had been dragged. Since my bedroom is upstairs, I had felt it safe to leave the window partly open. Like the rest of the country, Hampshire was enjoying a long hot spell, and there had been no rain for several weeks. The night air was heavy and still, and as I sat up in bed I became aware of the sweet, pungent smell of wood smoke. Then I heard the sound of dry timbers crackling and the neighing of the ponies in the paddock nearby.

When I reached the window, I could see tongues of flame running the entire length of the barn roof. They were leaping and dancing, scarlet against the black, impenetrable sky. Since the ponies' alarm was due to the smoke and the noise, and there was no livestock in the barn—only several hundred pounds' worth of hay for the winter feed—I decided against venturing forth into the night on any abortive rescue mission.

I telephoned the fire department, then dressed slowly, still in the darkness, watching the progress of the blaze as I pulled on my shirt and trousers. Fortunately the barn stood apart some distance from the main complex of buildings surrounding the house. There was no danger of anything else catching fire. Showers of sparks cascaded like bursting fireworks from the gutted roof, and now and then there was a crash as a beam burned through and went plunging inside the building.

As I watched the destruction I wondered if they were there even now, hidden in one of the hazel copses close to the hedge beside the barn. Were they waiting for me to come running from the house to deliver myself into their hands? I cheered myself a little by concluding that I wasn't quite as stupid as they believed to fall for such a blatant ruse. Only when I heard the heavy rumble of the fire engine

161

on the drive did I leave the house. In a way I was crediting them with more intelligence than they were prepared to grant me. Among the crowd of uniformed firemen at work around the barn I knew I was safe from the hidden rifle, the knife thrust, whatever end they had in mind for me.

The firemen turned their hoses on the barn, and within thirty minutes the flames were extinguished. As dawn broke they dealt with a last few smoldering pockets in various corners of the ruined building. The roof had completely collapsed, the red tiles lying in scorched heaps on the earthen floor. Charred beams were embedded in the ground, some of them driven deep by the force of their fall.

While the firemen put away their equipment I went around the walls searching for any sign of the intruders. But there was nothing. If there had been any footprints in the dust, there was now no dust, only mud trampled and rutted by pounding feet and the wheels of the fire truck. The senior fire officer made his own inspection and attributed the blaze to spontaneous combustion from the stored hay. He made some remark about this being a common hazard at the present time because of the exceptionally dry weather. I agreed, but knew better. It must have been an easy job; one match was all they would have needed.

≥ ≥ ≥

Later that day, after several hours of careful thought, I made a decision. Having already taken steps to safeguard Felicity and the children by sending them off to Spain, I now had no wish to endanger my property any further. For all I knew the house would be next. Sooner or later a confrontation was inevitable. I therefore decided to choose my own territory for such an encounter, a place that would give me every advantage because of my familiarity with the terrain, a place untrammeled by forests and secluded lanes like the countryside around my house. There was only one part of England that fulfilled both qualifications: the moorlands of Cumbria and Northumberland on either side of Hadrian's Wall.

I knew all the main parts of the Roman wall and the surrounding countryside, having walked along much of this region with Jonathan on one of his summer holidays from school. On another occasion we'd gone farther north for several days, wandering over the mountainous land straddling the border between England and Scotland. It was a forbidding place, even in the finest weather, threaded by narrow, rushing streams and deep gullies strewn with boulders, while spread across much of its face like an enormous green carpet was the forest of Kielder with its dark, sunless rides cut in swaths between row upon row of pine and spruce trees. In addition, I'd often spent angling holidays in the area as the guest of Henry Arkwright, the chairman of one of the companies with which my firm does business. He owns a large estate covering thousands of acres, pockmarked with farms and tiny villages, with fishing rights on two rivers, the Tyne and the North Tyne. I'd also stayed several times in the small town of Corbridge, sometimes when angling, now and then when traveling to and from Scotland on business trips.

In such countryside I could use my knowledge and familiarity to best advantage, not merely to outwit my adversaries but to reverse the odds in my favor and lure them to their own deaths. By now I knew it was hopeless even to think of attempting to keep one step ahead of them, of merely trying to stay alive. They had to die, or I would never again know any peace of mind. Up on the barren moors surrounding the wall I had a better chance of success. In the circumstances, it was a chance I was willing to take.

I telephoned Henry at his office in Newcastle. He was disappointed he would not be around to see me, as he was just on the point of leaving by ship for Norway. But, he said, I was free to fish his stretches of the Tyne and North Tyne for as long as I wished. Local rumor had it that a good run of sea trout were in both rivers at the present time; there was also the chance to catch a fine, fresh grilse. I thanked him and rang off. Minutes later I was on the telephone to a hotel in Corbridge. It was an expensive place, a favorite haunt of American tourists, but I'd stayed there twice before, finding it clean, efficiently run, with well-cooked, interesting food. A thin voice informed me that they were very busy; it was, after all, the height of the holiday season. There were several minutes of silence before the receptionist finally returned to say they did indeed

163

have a last-minute cancellation. I could have a room from the following day.

"For how long, sir?"

"A week. Possibly more. I can't be more definite. It depends on my success with the sea trout—and other things."

The distant voice laughed.

"Very well, sir. We'll hold the booking open for you for another week at least. You can decide later what you want to do."

My next telephone call was to a security firm. One of their services was to provide an around-the-clock watch on unoccupied property. I felt sure there would be no further trouble at home after my departure. Whoever was watching me seemed to know every move I made. Because of this I sensed they would be on my trail almost immediately. They would find me at Corbridge, on the river, on the wall itself—I'd no doubts on that score. All the same, I wanted to take no more risks by leaving the house unguarded except for Mrs. Tasker's daily visits.

The firm said they would allocate three men to the job, who would arrive, as requested, after breakfast the following morning. I went to the kitchen, where Mrs. Tasker was preparing my lunch and told her I was going away for a spell. I explained about the security guards, but in her usual fashion she said little, merely raising her eyebrows, and continued with her work.

I cabled to Felicity in Spain, explaining that I had to make a rushed business trip to Edinburgh, then for the remainder of the day, between bouts of packing clothes and arranging my fishing tackle, let my mind dwell on the task I had set myself. I spent some time cleaning and checking the most important part of my luggage, a Smith & Wesson .38 revolver I'd obtained some years ago on a visit to America. I'd kept it in the house with the idea of using it to frighten potential burglars. I'd never bothered, however, to put a bullet through the barrel. I'd always assumed that the sight of the thing, loaded or unloaded, would be sufficient for my purposes.

Furthermore, I'd never gotten around to obtaining a license for it. I'd taken a considerable risk in not doing so. At the time, I had had no conscious wish to hide the firearm from the authorities but had merely forgotten to apply for the certificate. Afterward it seemed too late to bother about it; I was certain I'd never be forced to use it. I have a shotgun in the house, which I've used from time to time for shooting rabbits and pigeons. I've always held a license for that. Now I counted my blessings that the revolver remained unlicensed. No record existed that could trace its ownership to me. I didn't have much ammunition for it, a couple of dozen bullets at most, but I didn't intend to go in for a shooting match with my opponents. When eventually I would have to use the revolver, I intended to use it not in defense but in a short, sharp counterattack. The cylinder held five bullets, more than enough.

In the early evening I took the revolver and some ammunition and went into a small wood of beech and oak on the far boundary of my ground. I fired several shots at some decayed branches. A few wood pigeons cracked up through the tops of the trees and flew across the fields of ripening grain. The sound of the shots echoed across the silent landscape, hazy and still from the day's heat. Anyone hearing them would assume I was shooting pigeons as, of course, I'd every right to do on my own land. On every occasion I fired I hit the target. I had not fired a revolver since my days as a member of a shooting club not long after leaving school; once acquired, shooting is a skill seldom forgotten.

When I left the house and drove through the village shortly after ten o'clock the following morning, the Smith & Wesson was snug in its holster beneath my jacket. Fortunately it had been designed to be carried in this fashion. With a two-inch barrel, it weighed no more than nineteen ounces; its overall length was a little over six inches. In its holster the .38 made no more bulge than the average wallet. I'd checked my appearance in a mirror several times before leaving the house and there was no sign of the revolver with my jacket either open or buttoned.

I knew I was taking a risk should for any reason a perceptive policeman stop my car and talk to me, but then I had lived for too long on the edge of risk; I would continue to do so until the revolver against my chest spat back at the men who had selected me for death.

165

≥ ≥ ≥

The drive to Corbridge, much of it on expressways, was uneventful. On one occasion, however, after having stopped for a time at a service station to buy gas and have a snack, I suspected I was being followed by a dark red Renault 4. As far as I could judge, there were two occupants. When I eased my car down the slip road leading back onto the expressway, the Renault appeared to swing out behind me almost immediately. At first I just glanced in the rear-view mirror, saw the car, and thought nothing more about it. Once back on the expressway, I traveled at a steady fifty miles per hour in the slow lane, and for several miles the Renault held back, a dark blotch on the ribbon of road each time I glanced in the mirror. Then, to my surprise, I found it starting to overtake. When it went past it was traveling so fast that I had no time to get a clear view of the driver and passenger. A bus overtook me almost immediately and I lost sight of the Renault. After it disappeared from view I dismissed my suspicions about it.

I left the expressway at Carlisle and drove through wooded valleys on a winding road running alongside the River Tyne until I reached Corbridge. The hotel, a long, low building which, proclaimed a plaque just inside the main door, had been built in the seventeenth century, was in the main street at the top of a hill. My bedroom was at the front with a clear view down the short, steep hill to a seven-arched stone bridge spanning the river. Double glazing on the windows helped reduce the continual noise of traffic, mainly trucks grinding up the hill or changing gear for the descent onto the bridge. On the opposite side of the street was a guesthouse, and in front of the building a cramped open space bounded by a low stone wall was used for parking.

Before going down to dinner I washed and changed, then rang for a whisky, which I drank while gazing at the view across the river. I'd been sitting at the window for several minutes watching the sun burning red behind the trees on the crest of a distant hill when some movement made me look at the front of the guesthouse.

A small green van was being parked in a narrow space between

166

two cars. The driver, a youngish man in white jeans and a blue shirt, got out and went to the rear of the van to check the distance he had left between his vehicle and the cars on either side. A stocky man wearing dark glasses, who I supposed was his companion, emerged from the guesthouse and nodded, then together they lifted a couple of suitcases out of the back of the van.

For some reason I kept staring at the two figures, watching them walk toward the guesthouse. Slowly the reason for my attention became apparent. It was not the green van and its occupants that drew my eyes across the road but the car parked on the right, next to the wall. It was a Renault—a dark red Renault 4. Of course, I had no reason for supposing this to be the same car that had followed and overtaken me on the expressway; after all, it is a popular model. Even as I gazed at it I realized there must be thousands exactly like it on the roads every day. But too many coincidences had occurred in the past concerning my vendetta with the Tengerakis family. As far as I was concerned, it was the same car. I tried to recall if it had been there when I had arrived at the hotel, but there was no way I could coax my brain into remembering.

After a meal in the dining room, alive with the sound of American voices relating the day's sightseeing on the Roman wall, I returned to my room. There, with the aid of two more whiskies, I kept watch on the small parking lot in front of the guesthouse. When daylight faded completely I was still able to see clearly in the light from a streetlamp on the pavement and another light shining above the main door. No one who emerged showed any particular interest in the red Renault.

≥ ≥ ≥

It was still there in the morning when I got out of bed and pulled back the curtains. When after breakfast I climbed the stairs to my bedroom to collect my fishing tackle and packed lunch, the Renault was the only vehicle in the parking lot. The green van that had been parked alongside was just pulling away, crossing the street to a filling station beside the hotel. My car was in a yard at the rear of the

167

building. To get onto the road that would take me toward Hadrian's Wall and the stretch of river on which I intended to fish, I had to drive past the side of the hotel. At the front, on the main street, I had to make a sharp right-hand turn. For no more than thirty seconds the guesthouse was visible as I swung the car out and around, sufficient time to see that the parking lot was empty. The Renault had gone.

I received such a shock that my foot momentarily slipped on the clutch pedal. My car gave a lurch, almost stalling the engine. There was a furious horn blast from a bus that had climbed the hill and turned off the main street directly behind me. I fumbled with the gears, lifted an arm in a half-hearted gesture of apology, then accelerated away. As I drove out of Corbridge I tried to concentrate on handling the car, but part of my mind remained focused on the mysterious red Renault and its equally mysterious occupants.

Any suspicion that my imagination was playing tricks on me vanished several hours later. It was early afternoon. I'd eaten my pork pie and sandwiches and emptied the flask of coffee while seated in the shade of a couple of stunted alders on the banks of the North Tyne. At this point the river ran close to Chesters, the site of a Roman fort and bathhouse built on the route taken by the wall. A short distance below the pool where I'd been fishing, the remains of a Roman bridge still stood on the opposite bank, the stonework of one pier rising from the gurgling water, the abutment clear and well preserved. Traces of the wall were also visible close to the far bank of the river, and I had a clear view of the site of the fort on a mound behind an array of ramshackle iron fences; the area of the bathhouse was marked in similar fashion about thirty yards downstream on the far side of the fort.

While I'd been eating I'd watched several dozen people arrive to visit the site, their cars grinding in low gear down the hill from the military road to park in a grassy field directly opposite me. Several of them were picnicking on the opposite bank farther upstream.

A hatch of flies swarmed out from the undergrowth. For several minutes I watched them leaping and dancing like rolling mist on the surface of the water, then I picked up my rod. Already the pool was a mass of ripples as the trout appeared, thrusting upward, feeding hungrily. I had brought a nine-foot split-cane trout rod with me, hoping that one of Henry Arkwright's grilse or sea trout might succumb to the temptations of a choice dry fly. There are few greater thrills for an angler than the ensuing battle when he hooks a fresh-run grilse or sea trout on a light rod designed for catching much smaller fish.

The pool was wide and easy to fish. In midstream toward the top a couple of rocks jutted above the water and sent swift currents flowing eagerly toward both banks. I made three casts toward the lower side of one of the rocks. As the Silver Butcher bobbed on the ripples traveling diagonally across the pool, I saw it vanish; the line tightened, reel screaming. I had hooked my first trout of the day. Several minutes later, after a sustained struggle, it was on the bank at my feet, a plump speckled fish around one pound. The flies continued to dance above the water, great clouds of them emerging from the foliage. For the next ten minutes or so I fished intently, using all the skill I could muster, dropping the fly into the center of the boils made by the rising trout. I hooked three more and landed two fish smaller than the first one but equally good fighters.

I was making a long cast to reach some rising fish close against an overhang on the far bank when my right foot slipped, throwing me off-balance. As I thrust my arms out to prevent myself from toppling into the river, the line whipped around the branch of a tree twenty feet behind me. It took several minutes to untangle it and straighten out the knots in the slender cast. I was checking the barb on the hook of the Silver Butcher and turning toward the river when I spotted a red Renault 4 entering the field where the cars were parked.

It was too far away for me to see clearly the faces of the two men who got out, but they could see me without difficulty. They stood among the wandering tourists and started to watch through binoculars. I tried to appear unconcerned and returned to the edge of the riverbank. I started to fish once again. But every time I glanced casually in their direction the binoculars were on me, masking either one face or the other. It was a comfort to feel the .38 against my chest, but nothing would happen that afternoon; of that I was certain. This spot was too crowded, too public, for what they had in mind.

After an hour I grew tired of their scrutiny, which they appeared to maintain for most of the time, stopping only to mingle with the visitors walking around the site of the fort and baths. Once, they even came to the Roman bridge and looked upstream toward where I was fishing perhaps forty yards away. For the first time I could see them clearly—two stocky figures in dark trousers and white open-necked shirts. The one holding the binoculars was almost bald, stout, probably middle-aged, but his companion appeared to be in his twenties and had longish black hair. In a way he reminded me of Stephanides.

The older man laughed, the sound mocking me above the bubbling of the water. His companion muttered a reply, then spat into the river. They turned away and walked slowly through a group of shrieking children running down the slope toward the bridge. One youngster, a boy, bumped into the older man and fell over. The man helped him to his feet, ruffled his hair, and the boy ran off to join his companions. As far as I could see they did not glance in my direction again. They got into their car, and I went on watching as the red Renault turned out of the field and started to climb the hill toward the main road. Forty minutes later, when I returned to my hotel, the Renault was back in its original place, close to the wall in front of the guesthouse.

That evening I decided it was time to take the initiative, to draw them out into the open and show my hand. Their speed in following me to Corbridge, the ease with which they seemed to follow my every move, amazed me. I was convinced that very soon their game of stalking and taunting me would become tiresome to them. When that happened they would move swiftly to make their kill. I could only prevent this by moving first, just as swiftly and with as much cunning, so expertly that they would follow like sheep, unaware of the trap their prey had set.

Already in the last couple of days, since the idea of coming to Northumberland had entered my head, I had chosen the spot; I'd gone over the intricate details again and again, working and reworking them until I had a clear understanding of every aspect, an awareness of every possibility.

Tonight it was like some game of chess played in the mind, each

170

move analyzed and interpreted. Tomorrow it would no longer be a game.

As I prepared for bed I looked across the street and thought of the pawns in my game, somewhere behind the gray stone walls and high windows of the guesthouse. Were they too looking out, staring at the hotel? Were they at this very moment thinking of me? Planning their move against me, their pawn?

≥ ≥ ≥

When I drove away from the hotel shortly after nine thirty the following morning, a light drizzle spotted the windshield. Corbridge looked gray, the stonework of the buildings matching the mood of the weather. The Renault was still parked in front of the guesthouse, and I caught a glimpse of two figures on the porch. It might have been them; I couldn't be sure. I didn't care very much, because really it didn't matter. As I left Corbridge I knew enough about their tactics to know they would follow and find me. They had shown time and again an uncanny ability to know everything I did. It was as well, I considered, that they could not read what went on in my mind; thought appeared to be the last vestige of privacy remaining to me.

I felt a tingle of anticipation, a glow of excitement deep within my body, as I drove up the hill toward the junction with the military road. At least for the moment there was no fear gnawing at me, not even a glimmer of apprehension at the possible outcome if my scheme proved reckless. I was buoyant with thoughts of success, with little time or inclination to dwell on the possible dangers. After all, as I had asked myself the previous evening, what had I to lose? Do nothing, and certainly die; do something, and possibly survive. I was fully prepared to gamble on the slender odds.

I followed a cattle truck belching black smoke from its exhaust until I reached the road junction. Fortunately it was going to the right, toward Newcastle. Ahead of me was the road to the Scottish border. I turned left toward Carlisle. The rain was heavier now, blown by a strengthening wind and spattering in wild flurries against the windshield. I switched on the wipers, not caring much about the

171

weather. I had my anorak with me, lying on the back seat, and stout walking boots on my feet. In a way the rain—and judging by the heavy overcast sky it had set in for the day—suited my purposes.

In the distance to my right, beyond the clumps of gorse and the sour green fields with their flocks of grazing sheep, the dry-stone walls and the isolated clumps of gale-ravaged trees, was mile upon mile of open moorland. Already I could see the mist hanging over it like a shroud. Out there, far beyond the route of the wall, I could use the weather to my advantage, joining this to my familiarity with the terrain. At this very moment I expected my adversaries from their island of sun would be cursing the vagaries of the English climate, the sudden change overnight from heat and sun to cold and torrential rain. I could only hope that today of all days, when my mind and body were geared to setting the pace, they would not decide to lie low because of the weather. For a time as I drove along the road, with its long, straight stretches following a route laid down in Roman times, I felt as though I were treading a tightrope, eager now for the gloomy day and the actions I proposed to take, almost praying for the right balance in the weather so that the hunters would follow without further delay.

I turned off the road and into a large parking lot. At one corner stood a trailer with the word *Information* painted on its side. Beside it was a signpost pointing the way through a gate in the stone wall along a footpath winding across the fields to Housesteads Fort. The fort was almost a mile away, but despite the rain it was possible to see the wall running along a ridge on either side of the excavations on the site of the fort. I had several reasons for choosing this spot to be my starting point, the place where, like a fox, I would lay my false scent.

Of all the excavated sites on the wall, Housesteads attracts the greatest number of visitors. For several miles on either side the wall had been restored so that there were always people pacing along the top where it soared up and down following the crest of the crags. I intended to wander through the fort, get onto the wall, then after a couple of miles leave it and cut across the moorland to the spot I had in mind for my ambush.

Despite the mist and rain there were already about a dozen cars in the lot as well as a large van and a bus. As I locked my car two tourist buses arrived. On the path between the parking lot and the fort were numerous figures, alone, in pairs, or in huddled groups, plastic raincoats flapping in the wind, heads lowered against the scudding rain. Initially, in the early stages of my journey, I would be in the company of dozens of people; as a result, later, if the necessity ever arose I doubted if anyone would remember me as any different from all the others. Certainly there were many more isolated and remote places in the district that I could have chosen, but in all of them I carried the risk of being spotted by a hiker or camper, solitary people who would be certain to recall the intrusive presence of another stranger. Here for a time I would be part of the herd, anonymous, ignored, and unnoticed, a welcome anonymity that would also be granted to the two men who were now, I hoped, not far behind me on the road along which I had just driven.

I had to turn up the collar of my anorak against the rain as I walked across the fields. There were a farmhouse and some outbuildings beside the site of the fort and arrow-shaped signs directing the way to an iron-roofed building housing a museum of relics found during the excavations. I bought an admission ticket to the site and stood for a time in the doorway of the museum staring through the curtain of mist toward the road.

I must have been there for ten minutes dodging from side to side to allow people to enter and leave. It was both awkward and uncomfortable. One newly arrived visitor shook out her umbrella and showered me with rain water. There was no apology. I glared at her; she glared back, then in a loud voice commanded three sullen-looking children trailing up the hill, "Hurry up—we really do have so much to see and do today." But I stuck to my spot in the narrow doorway, unwilling to get wet before I had proof of what I wanted to see.

When the red Renault did come into view it was a tiny blob of color among the other vehicles in the parking lot. I waited until I saw two figures emerge and start to walk toward the gate in the wall, mere specks against the gray landscape; then I stepped out of the

173

museum and made my way through the mud to the enclosure surrounding the site of the fort.

For several minutes I wandered around, mingling with the visitors on the network of paths between bathhouse, granary, barracks, and stores. The stonework, parts of walls, flooring, all gleamed wet in the rain. There was a grassy mound in the center of the complex and I stood on it, looking around the site, appearing to assess size and shape while really I was keeping watch on the approaching figures climbing the hill.

I saw them walk past the farmhouse. The younger one was smoking a cigarette. He waited outside the museum while his companion went inside, presumably to buy the tickets that would admit them to the site. When he reappeared he was smiling. The younger one said something and they both laughed; then I saw them looking across the face of the slope to where I stood on the mound. I looked slowly away and for several seconds watched a family trying to take photographs of one another perched on top of the wall. When I allowed my eyes to look once again in the direction of the two figures, the younger one was grinding the cigarette butt beneath his heel and they were walking side by side toward the entrance to the fort.

I waited until they momentarily disappeared from view in a dip in the ground before I started to walk toward the wall. Worn steps led up to it, and when I had climbed them I was on top, hundreds of feet above the plain looking north across the moorland toward the Wark and Kielder forests. Beyond, somewhere behind the haze of rain and mist, was the invisible Scottish border running among the peaks of the Cheviot Hills. I stood looking, with the rain and wind on my face just as countless thousands of Roman soldiers must have done centuries before me.

I could feel my heart pounding as I turned to the left and walked along the broad stone slabs spanning the wall. I entered a long, narrow strip of larch and pine trees growing on either side, those on my right rising sheer from the uppermost face of the cliff, their branches interlocking above my head. Among the foliage the wind made a rushing sound like the ebbing tide on a shingle beach. A crow flap-

174

ped off, cawing its alarm at my approach. The tension now started to take hold of me, tightening around my body as if my chest were being constricted by some giant hand. Within the next ten minutes or so, if my adversaries continued to follow, I would know I had succeeded; after that it would be easy to lure them away to the spot of my choice. If, however, they hung back and allowed me to walk on alone, my efforts would have been wasted. There would be one more day to wait, twenty-four more hours of intolerable suspense.

I halted in the middle of the wood, fingering the collar of my anorak, pulling it tighter around my neck. At the same time I half turned and looked back. They were about a hundred yards away, in full view on top of the wall. I noticed the vivid red of the younger one's anorak in contrast to the more sober blue of his companion's raincoat. He would make an easy target out there among the boulders beside the lake.

When I set off once again I began to walk purposefully, no longer content to saunter. I wanted to convey a picture of a man taking strenuous exercise with little concern for his surroundings. My strides grew longer, and I was forced to break them only occasionally when I met groups of people returning toward Housesteads from Milecastle, a well-preserved garrison compound, one of several along the length of the wall.

As I left the shelter of the wood, the full force of the wind struck me, almost throwing me off-balance. Flurries of rain beat against the side of my head. Above me the clouds seemed very close, great swollen masses of black and gray drooping in the sky. I went past the Milecastle enclosure, where people were sheltering in the lee of the wall.

The wall was now running downhill and I was striding effortlessly, being forced on at too great a speed. Once or twice my boots slipped on the stones and I almost fell over the edge. Then the cliff with its narrow ridge was left behind and the wall took a sudden turn to the right, plunging at an angle before going sharply up to the left to climb yet another hill. In the L-shaped cleft was a gap to allow sheep to pass through and on the right, in a gentle slope lead-

175

ing onto the moorland, was a large stone-walled enclosure where a shepherd could gather his flock together for dipping or counting and where the animals could take shelter during a storm.

I jumped off the wall and into the grass, squelching my way across the sheep droppings toward a gate on the far side. A couple of sheep, lying against a mound of rocks, rose to their feet as I passed. They ran bleating, short tails bobbing, and I took the opportunity while watching them to glance up at the ridge. My pursuers were now passing Milecastle, twin figures etched against the stormy sky, plodding on along the wall, still intent on following me.

≥ ≥ ≥

I climbed the gate and went down the last part of the slope almost at a trot. I knew this part of the countryside was private property, so from now on the likelihood of meeting anyone was fairly remote. About four miles away, directly ahead, was the Wark Forest. The space between the forest and where I was now standing appeared at first glance to be flat open country. But I knew that in the intervening space were numerous gullies and boulder-strewn folds through which ran narrow, turbulent streams. And in the middle of it all was a small lake with sheer sides, where the water was black, even on the brightest summer's day, because of its depth and the high content of peat. It was toward this spot that I headed.

There was no proper walking path, but out of the maze of paths used by the sheep to crisscross the moor there was one main route. It must have been there for a century, so battered had the earth become from the animals' trotters. I had used it on several occasions during holidays in the district and always found it easy to follow in any weather. Now, as I glanced back and saw the two men hurrying through the sheep enclosure, I felt a further surge of confidence.

I strode on at a steady pace. Away from the ridge and the top of the crags the strength of the wind had eased a little. The rain seemed to fall of its own momentum, no longer slapping my face. But the mist was still there all around, about two hundred yards away, swirling like escaping steam above the undulating moor.

I was well aware that the next couple of miles would be crucial. If

176

the mist kept its distance I could continue to count on it as an ally. I now had to pace myself correctly, to keep far enough away from the pair following me to be safe from them, but not too far in case they might lose sight of me. At the same time, I needed a reasonable field of vision. I watched the mist creeping forward, hoping it would keep away. At least the rain was persistent, soaking my hair, trickling down my neck; my trouser legs were sodden from the slap of wet grass and heather. I cheered myself a little by reflecting that any discomfort I was experiencing was no doubt being felt to a greater degree by my adversaries.

I strode on, hearing the rushing of the water in two streams as they emptied into the lake, the incessant sound drawing closer minute by minute. The silence of my thoughts was broken only by this sound and the occasional screech of a lapwing wheeling in the wind above the desolate moorland.

The sheep track went around in a semicircle before entering a gully about fifty yards wide and two hundred yards long that opened out to reveal the lake and the rain-swollen streams pouring over the rocks. For perhaps three minutes I would be out of sight. Already, as I looked behind me, the pair were hidden by an outcrop of rock. I started to run, dodging between the boulders, not bothering to follow the path, trying to get as close as possible to the lake before finding a spot in which to hide. I looked back several times; I was still on my own.

My heart was thumping, my shirt was soaked with sweat, and my legs were aching when I saw the ideal place—a large rock with a flat top, smooth as a table, surrounded on two sides by mounds of smaller boulders. I cut off to my right and scrambled up the incline until I reached the rock. When I threw myself down behind it I startled a hare sleeping in a tussock of grass. The animal bolted, long ears flat against its back. I flopped onto the ground and lay still, gulping air into my lungs, my limbs trembling.

I found I was completely concealed behind the rock and its neighboring boulders, and when I raised myself onto my knees and looked over the top, there in the distance were the two men. They were standing close together at the narrow entrance to the gully.

177

One of them was pointing in the direction of the lake while the other shielded his eyes from the rain and tried to catch sight of me.

Instinct told me they'd never give up now; they had come too far. I was also fairly certain my momentary disappearance would not cause suspicion. By now they would be able to appreciate the problems involved in maintaining a constant watch amid such difficult countryside. When I saw them start to pick their way among the rocks, following the sheep path toward the lake, I knew I was correct on both counts. They were hurrying, no doubt fearful of losing me completely, but as they drew closer I could see their hands were empty. The older one carried the binoculars in a case hanging from a strap slung around his neck.

I pulled the zipper on the front of my anorak and reached inside, releasing the .38 from its holster. The cylinder was full—five bullets. I was certain I could succeed with two quick shots. If necessary I stood every chance of hitting and killing at a range of fifty yards. But I wanted my targets much closer than that. Not only did I want to be assured of success before I pulled the trigger, but in a perverse fashion I wanted them both within clear sight of me so that I could observe their reactions. I wanted to see the expressions of terror on their faces, feel their momentary spasms of fear as the bullets struck home, and in that split second announce that I had trapped them. They had terrorized me far beyond the normal limits of endurance. I wanted one brief moment to implant the fear that had been mine into their own unguarded bodies, one moment when I could witness their horror.

I ticked off the distance: fifty yards, forty, thirty . . .

For a moment I thought of allowing them to go on by, then shooting them both in the back. But the thought passed and the .38 was resting against the rock aimed at the chest of the older man.

Twenty yards . . .

My hands trembled a little. The inside of my mouth was so dry that my tongue scraped against the back of my teeth.

Fifteen yards . . .

Any moment. Closer. Still closer . . .

Ten yards . . .

178

I fired.

The bullet went into the older man's chest, slicing through the strap of the binocular case. He jerked backward, clawing at the front of his raincoat. For a moment it almost looked as though he was trying to prevent the binoculars from falling to the ground. He toppled over, landing on his back across a boulder. There was no sound, only a few spasms from legs and arms, then stillness.

The thrill of success made me rash. The confidence surging inside me pushed my body up so that when I fired at the younger man he would see my head and shoulders, be aware of my triumph. I raised myself above the level of the rock, my finger already starting to squeeze the trigger. I failed to appreciate the instantaneous reactions that can come to a young, fit man with only seconds to warn him of death.

As I fired he was already throwing his body to one side. I saw the bullet strike a rock close to his left leg and heard the whine of the ricochet echoing through the gully. I fired again and he was rolling over and over along the ground, tumbling and crouching like a cat. When he came around to face me he had an automatic pistol in his right hand. With his first shot I felt a searing pain at the top of my left shoulder, the bullet cutting a furrow through the padding in my anorak. I ducked and his second shot sent chips of rock across the top of my head. A shower of fine dust fell onto my damp hair. Some of it went into my eyes, temporarily blinding me. I rubbed at them with my free hand, feeling them raw and tender, smarting painfully. When I looked around the side of the rock my vision was clouded as if the mist had descended unnoticed to envelop my body in a haze.

He was running now, dodging and weaving from side to side, climbing the opposite face of the gully. Within seconds he would be out of sight, out of range. I fired again, feeling a surge of relief as the bullet struck his right ankle, pitching him over onto his side. He started to crawl toward a small mound of rocks. I stood up and took careful aim. My final bullet seemed to lift him clear of the ground. I saw his pistol spinning into a tussock of grass. He lay quite still, one arm outstretched, fingers curled around one of the rocks from which he had sought shelter

The silence was acute. It was almost possible to hear the rain striking the rocks. From somewhere far beyond the fringes of the mist came the bleating of sheep.

When I reached the body I saw my bullet had entered his back directly behind his heart. Silently I cursed myself for my earlier reluctance to shoot a man in the back, my stupid desire to wring every shred of triumph from my dominance. There was no triumph in me now, merely fear because in my ineptitude I had allowed so many shots to be fired and thus increased the risk of discovery.

I started to work quickly. Fear and the delayed reaction of shock obliterated any awareness of the outside world, set my body working mechanically, almost desperately. I dragged both bodies to the edge of the lake, then darted back and forth collecting rocks and small stones. I filled their pockets with the rocks and stuffed them between their clothes. And when I could do no more, I toppled each body in turn into the lake. They sank immediately, causing no more than a slight tremor on the surface of the black, peaty water. I pitched in the younger man's automatic pistol and the binoculars in their case. There were a couple of splashes, a few ripples, and then they too were gone.

When I straightened up and looked around me I realized the rain was still falling relentlessly. The mist was much closer, silent, impenetrable. And I was alone with only my memories. There was a dull pain in my left shoulder and the cloying touch of blood on my arm. Inside I felt quite cold, almost numbed. There was, just as before, no exhilaration, no pounding feeling of elation. Instead, deep inside my brain was a fragment of reason, a mere kernel of awareness, pinpointing the futility of the vendetta I had set in motion— the vendetta that had led me to kill and had driven others to want to kill me.

⩾ ⩾ ⩾

As I started to retrace my steps along the gully a new fear took hold of me, a chilling realization that I had been corrupted by my desire to seek revenge for Jonathan's murder. I had planned things, accomplished deeds, which at one time I would never have believed myself capable of even thinking about, let alone doing. Somehow, the evil of the three Tengerakis brothers had infected my soul, had developed within me a ruthless cunning so treacherous that the thought sickened me. Had I in some way become unbalanced by my search for revenge? Was I, having taken the law into my own hands, no better than the thugs I had killed?

Perhaps most terrifying was the slow, almost paralyzing realization that I had started a chain of events that at some stage in the future I would no longer be able to control. Two men had come to England to kill me; now they were dead. But would others take their place? Others who would haunt me as before, watching, waiting? Next month? Next year? And for how long would I be able to continue resisting them? Would there come a time when the will to fight back was gone, when every shred of self-preservation was peeled and stripped away and I no longer cared?

I think it was when I had climbed the hill and reached the ridge along which the Roman wall stretched away into the distance and the wind once again sent the rain lashing against my body that the moment of truth washed over me. I halted, staring with glazed eyes at the bleakness of the surrounding countryside, the distant hills obscured by the rain, the mist creeping forward to envelop the grazing sheep, now only shapeless forms in the rough pasture far below. I knew then, with an awful sense of finality, that I was trapped by a web of circumstance. I had allowed myself to be seduced by a blood lust, ensnared in a vendetta that now meant a life to be lived on the threshold of fear.

Later, in my hotel room, as I washed the flesh wound on my shoulder, I considered that five men had died as a result of my vendetta—and Maria, who had also had cause to hate. But, I asked myself, was her desire for vengeance merely enflamed by my own enthusiasm and determination? Had I, by drawing her into the search for vengeance, been responsible for her death? Was any man's life—even that of my own brother—worth the chain of revenge I had forged?

181

≥ ≥ ≥

I can never know the answers—not now. They must forever remain as enigmatic as my own future, a future blighted by a curse spawned from my own soul.

Perhaps one day you will read in your newspaper a brief account of my death. When you do, I am certain it will be described either as an accident or, if by some act of violence, as a total mystery. Such mystery, after all, is the hallmark of death by vendetta, the imprint of the secret hatred that burns within the body of those held in its grip.

Hate has the power to destroy a man, totally consume him. Only the culmination of the vendetta can extinguish it completely.